Jack in the Blood: The Book of Ancestors

To Tracey

Lots of love,

Jaine x.

Jack in the Blood: The Book of Ancestors

Written and illustrated by Jason Buck

Jason Buck
2017

First Printing: 2017

ISBN 978-0-244-01428-5

www.JasonBuckStoryteller.co.uk

www.Facebook.com/JasonBuckStoryteller

Contents

Acknowledgements

There are a number of people who've helped me with this collection of stories, either with expertise in certain fields, or just with simple inspiration and I'd like to thank them here...

Ruth Fillery-Davis for being, in her own words "a raging Roman nerd" and bringing some structure and reality to Jacobus' position in the Roman Army and how the group he was sent to Carthage with might have been formed in "The Brothers and The Stone".

Fal Carmichael and chum Zuzana Krchova for the Bohemian / Czech names in "Child of the Seasons (Part 2)", especially 'Zimolezka' – 'Little Honeysuckle'.

Phil Clayton for expertise in all things charcoal, and Nina Hansen, following a conversation about trolls, for introducing me to the mysterious Hulder, all of which appear in "The Hooked Horror and the Forest Girl".

My late mother and various aunts and uncles, for information about the very real Rupert Simms, who is responsible for covering up "The Clay Dragon of Staffordshire".

My Uncle Jack for the information that ultimately created Private Buck in "Four Knaves".

Finally, Mike Rogers, who not only continues to mentor and guide me as a storyteller, but also corrected my inadequate Anglo Saxon Latin in "The Angel's Feather", and also in "The Brothers and The Stone", and provided the final line on the final page of this collection.

Forward

In 2016 Jason had his DNA tested to find out where his ancestors came from. Even though the results were not as exotic as he'd hoped for, it told a story of how he, a white Englishman, was the descendant of many, many generations of people who had been born, lived, had had children and moved around many, many different countries.

Already enjoying the diverse and colourful mythologies from around the world, and living in a time of global movementof huge numbers of people, whether escaping conflict, environmental change, or simply having access to the global community, this inspired Jason to produce a collection of original stories, creating a narrative from his ancestors – some real (you can find them on a simple internet search), some imagined as to how he came to be the person he is, born and living in the country he's found in today.

Some of the stories refer to well-known places, creatures, beliefs histories and mythologies, and some are brand new, but fitted to the times and places they are set.

The 'Jack in the Blood' collection was written to entertain and to challenge more rigid ideas of cultural and national identity, within a context of a wider view of time.

Prologue

J ack.

Jackrabbit; Jack knife; Jackass; Jack-of-all-trades … master of none.

Jack and the Beanstalk; Jack the Giant Killer; Jack - the Knave of Hearts, he stole those tarts, and took them clean away.

Jackanapes; car jack; Natterjack … toad. Jackhammer; Jolly Jack Tar; Jack in the box; Jack in the Green?

Jack in the blood; Jack across countries; Jack across oceans; Jack, down through the years and across the centuries: Jack until today.

My name is Jack.

But of course, it isn't and you know that; but my family has a name that has been passed down through the years. And it's Jack.

My father's father and his father before him and so on have been named William and this is the name on their birth certificates, on their tombs and even on plaques on city walls: William; but that was not the name they were known by.

They were known as Jack.

Why? I didn't know. Maybe you know. But I needed to know; I needed to find out.

* * *

Have you ever been *called* to a place?

Called, like you need to be somewhere and you *must* go there?

Called and you don't know by who or what, but you *know* that you need to go there … even if you're not quite sure where *there* is?

I was.

"Jack", said the feeling that pulled and tugged at the edges of my thoughts, at the edges of my dreams. "Come back to me, Jack, and tell me what you have seen and heard and learned. It's time to come back to me Jack, and bring me the stories in your blood".

So I went.

I opened my laptop and I began to search the internet for places to go. I looked on websites for plane tickets but each time I tried all the flights were booked: *all* of them.

I searched for tickets to Africa, but all the flights were booked.

I searched for tickets to America, but all the flights were booked.

I searched for tickets to Thailand, but all the flights were booked.

I searched for tickets to Australia, to New Zealand, to Russia, to Brazil, to Tonga, to Egypt, to Scotland, to Ireland, to Iceland, to France to Germany, to Switzerland … and they were all booked. All of them.

And then I found a flight to Italy. One flight.

* * *

I landed at Aeroporto Venezia – at Venice Airport – and then, escaping the dry and will-sapping heat, I gratefully climbed inside my tiny hire car and drove south.

I drove for two hours along roads that kept their distance from old volcanoes, dotting the skyline with peaks and dips like a heartbeat, their sides studded with vineyards and blanketed with dry soil.

I stopped at a service station for food, nervous about trying the few words I had learned on the flight, but excited, hoping for an Italian delicacy, only to be disappointed at the tubes of Pringles and plastic bottles of Coke next to limp slices of pizza and trays of American muffins.

So I drove on, *still* not knowing where I was going; only heading towards the pull, towards the feeling, towards, "Jack. Come back to me now. Come back to me, Jack, and tell me what you found".

Turning off the motorway in the region of Vicenza, the road was narrow, winding, flanked by fields of maize growing thick, and leafy, taller than a man, watered with fountain-sprinklers that slowly turned in the baking sun, drenching the ground and giving a waxy shine to the deep green, sword-blade leaves.

I drove through a small town with buildings of brick and yellow stone, terracotta pan-tiled roofs and indiscernible shop signs that yet stirred distant memories of dreams before my birth.

And then I reached a villa: Once grand, but still beautiful in its slow decay. Stepping from the car the air was arid and still, insects stirred in dry grassy banks, swifts shrieked high in the deep blue and my shirt stuck to my body, while a combine harvester thrummed angrily in the hot and heavy distance.

This was the place. This was where I had been called.

And then she who had called me, had called me Jack, called me across the miles, opened the door to her villa and I stepped into the cool.

The woman's name was Kleiou, but I already knew that.

She was timeless; impossible to age – both young and old. Beautiful and graceful, I heard her speech in my head and in my heart, understanding that while my ears heard words I didn't understand, their sounds drifted into meaning in my core, and I was humbled and gentled, like a kitten, in the presence of her authority, her kindness and the unspoken power that poured from her like heat from a sunbaked rock.

The villa was cool and dim, after the blinding light of the Italian summer sun. She invited me to sit in a comfortable, well-upholstered wingback chair, and handed me a ceramic goblet. It looked Greek in origin, as I knew she was, and it was filled with wine as rich-red in colour and iron-scented as blood.

As I drank a deep draught of the thick, sweet wine, I looked around the room: The walls were a plain mustard yellow, the rustic unevenness of their plastering at odds with the beautifully and skilfully crafted, glass-fronted frames that dotted the walls, containing parchments, papyrus and papers, all with delicately calligraphed scripts in languages ancient and modern, and beautifully illuminated pictures of battles, grand meetings, deaths, births, people, animals and some a mixture of both.

Then the wine woke voices in my blood: The voices of my forefathers and mothers of old. They spoke to me from over the centuries and told me stories that ridiculed the idea of national boundaries, revealing them to be only as real and as fixed as the shifting dunes of the desert, and how our overweening, individualistic pride rises Priapicly, only to droop, in time, and be trodden under the boot of those hurrying to take our place. They spoke to me and showed me hate and greed, violence and selfishness and all the ugliness of us naked apes.

And then, at the edge of hopelessness I saw a light. Only a wink at first, like sunlight catching a fragment of forgotten, broken, unswept glass, but then the light became a glow as the memories unfolded and cascaded and unravelled like golden thread spun from straw, and the ugly stories turned to tales of love, to stories where magic and incredible creatures were real, of heroes and heroines and struggle and triumph, of hope and stories of Jack … Jack down the years, Jack down the centuries; stories that had taken nearly two thousand years to be made, and all from one point.

And as my eyes drooped and my memory stretched back down the years I found a voice and I started to speak, started at the beginning, and told my Muse the first of the stories – of the first Jack in the blood … in my blood.

ΚΛΕΙΩ

Κλειω (Kleiou), Vincentia, Roman Italy

At thirteen Jacobus was almost an adult, and he would soon be expected to take on some of the duties that would earn his keep, improve his family's finances and, ultimately, set him up as an independent man with prospects.

Born in the Greek city of Thespiae, near mount Helicon, in the year 165CE, his parents had moved to Rome and then onto Vincentia when he was still a baby. A skilled mathematician, his father had become tutor to the sons of a number of wealthy houses in the area, running a small school, in the Greek style.

Having inherited his mother and father's sharp intellect, Jacobus enjoyed studying, and dreaming of new inventions that he would one day make. His chief interests were mathematics and history and he was happy to spend time reading and re-reading manuscripts detailing great historical events, or listening to the storytellers, relating the old legends, especially when it came to those of his motherland where Gods changed the fates of mortals, satyrs frolicked around Muses, and wise and learned centaurs studied the movements of the heavens.

However, his bookishness, calm wit, foreign birth and lean build made him a target for the local churls and bullies. They said he was a dirty immigrant; they said he wasn't a true Roman, called him a boy-lover and would chase him, throwing stones and, if they caught him, throwing him to the ground, punching and kicking him before wandering away, laughing among themselves at their superiority.

The more this happened the more Jacobus withdrew from the company of those his age, and the deeper he buried himself in legends and histories – places where he could imagine himself as the conquering hero or the magnanimous king.

Of course, he couldn't avoid the village bullies all the time and one day he was running an errand for his parents when he spotted a knot of the intellectually clumsy but hard-fisted boys and decided to leave the familiar path he walked most days and climb up through the hills to avoid them. Creeping through the dry grasses and weaving through vineyards, he didn't realise he'd been spotted and that, as he was starting to enjoy what was for him an adventurous exploration, the group of bullies was stalking him, advancing quickly on his trail.

Thinking he'd escaped detection, Jacobus stopped on a hilltop to inspect some ruins he'd not noticed before. Not being an independent youth, he never strayed far from home on his own; on this occasion, however, he was warming to his newfound freedom. On the hilltop were the remains of what must have been a shrine of sorts, but it was difficult to tell to whom the shrine was dedicated. Underneath a dry-barked cypress lay a tumble of carved stone; some of the slabs had once been walls and on these were carved lyres and scrolls.

Jacobus was so absorbed in tracing the faded and weathered lines of these old carvings he didn't hear the boys creeping closer until they were almost upon him: The snapping of a parched twig jerked him alert and, spinning round, he found himself in a circle of wolves – the village boys had trapped him.

At a shout from the biggest and oldest of them they descended on him. He had no time to run, no time to defend himself, only time to curl into a ball as he was viciously knocked to the ground, bringing his arms up to cover his head and face. Amidst the pain and the fear, and the jeers and laughter from his abusers, he called out in his mother tongue, impotently shouting curses and calling for the Gods to save him and strike down his attackers.

Of course no one was struck down and he was not magically transported, but in the middle of the melee what seemed like a miracle did happen. A woman's voice, strong, authoritative, cultured and stentorian in its delivery plunged like a sword blade into the heart of the fray and brought it to an immediate stop.

"What is the meaning of this?! This land belongs to me and I will have no violence and no blood spilled by anyone, without my authority!"

The boys had stopped their attack and Jacobus peered out from between his arms to see what was happening.

A noblewoman was standing by the tumbled stones he had been looking at a few moments earlier. She was swathed in rich fabric, her hair had been set in a fashionable and expensive way and she stared imperiously at the group. Silence held everyone, as the village boys didn't know what to do, suddenly outclassed by this unfamiliar noblewoman.

All she did was step forward and make a loud *HISSSSS!* The boys scattered, leaving Jacobus struggling to his feet, spluttering to apologise – although for what he wasn't sure. As he stood up the world felt like it tilted and slid away and he found himself sitting hard on the ground again.

"Sit still, young Jacobus", said the woman, kindly, and through a mixture of his spinning head and her natural authority he had no choice. She knelt and dabbed a corner of her robe on his forehead and he saw blood. Putting his hand to his head he found the wound, sticky and painful, and saw how there was also blood on the corner of one of the ruined stones which he must have hit as he fell. Trying to talk, he found the words wouldn't come out properly and the woman hushed him and tended to his wound.

"I know you, Jacobus. I know who you are and who you will be, Jack. I know how you spend your time with the stories and histories of this world and others. I am Kleiou – the Muse of History – and this place is sacred to me". He had seen pictures of her – of course, her symbols: the lyre, to accompany the bards in storytelling, and the scroll, to record the histories – that's why they were carved on these stones.

"Those boys who attacked you by my shrine will be punished", she continued. "By their families, yes, but also by History, for their names will be forgotten even before their deaths. But, for you, Jack – I will give you and your descendants good lives and then, in two thousand years, they must return to me and bring me their stories in your blood. Go and travel the world and let your children and your children's children travel yet further and see the wonders that are now and that are yet to come. But for now, Jack, sleep now, Jack, and come back to me later – much later – with stories, carried in your blood".

* * *

When Jacobus woke it was almost dark. His head thumped painfully, but his mind had cleared from earlier in the day. He was sprawled next to pile of ruined stones from the shrine to Kleiou, the Muse of History, and someone, not far away was shouting his name. Painfully, he answered and moments later a number of lanterns appeared, bobbing over the brow of the hill – a group, led by his father, had come to find him.

It appeared that the village boys had ambushed him, but during the struggle, Jacobus had fallen and hit his head on some rubble that was lying thereabouts. Thinking he had been killed, the boys ran away in fright, swearing each other to secrecy. But when he didn't return, and his Father had gone from house to house to see if he could find where he was, one of the boys broke down and the awful story came tumbling out.

Thankfully for the boys, Jacobus was *not* dead, merely concussed, and the boys got away with beatings for attacking the son of a ranking family, rather than anything more serious or final.

Jacobus was seen to by the physic, but, apart from the outlandish hallucination he reported, concerning the appearance of a Muse, the prognosis was a complete recovery after some bed rest, red meat and motherly love.

And so, Jacobus, the first Jack in a line of many returned to his everyday life, but always, at the back of his mind, and often in dreams was his meeting with Kleiou – real or imagined – and he, and his descendants, embarked on a life of travel and adventure.

The Brothers and The Stone, Ruins of Carthage [Tunisia]

Today, if were you travel to North Africa, to Tunisia, in the most north easterly part you might find the remains of the once-mighty city of Carthage.

Populated by North Africans and Southern Europeans, it resisted but was finally destroyed by the Roman Empire and the city was raised to the ground.

As you looked at the scattered, shattered marble and hoped to find the face of a wonderful statue of a mythical beast peering up from the sand, it would be quite understandable that, by that banks of a small river, next to an insignificant bridge made of modern rolled steel, you might miss what may appear to be an equally insignificant pile of cut stone, part of a long since tumbled down pillar for an ancient bridge, now weathered and worn by wind and water.

But if you were able to take a boat out to inspect it, you might still be able to make out a carving of a lyre and a scroll – the maker's mark, perhaps – and the words 'Jacobus Artifex Construxit', and that it appears to have a curious hole bored into it, from the top, almost all the way to the bottom – if you were able to see.

If you were to search for records of this pile of stones you would find none; and if you were to ask the local people what it was, they would tell you that, yes it was once part of a bridge in ancient times, and that it must never be disturbed or moved, but that is all they know.

So I will tell you what it is and why it was built and, most importantly, why it must never be disturbed.

Even many years after the city of Carthage was destroyed there was still plunder to be had and, at that time, there was none more efficient at plundering than the war machine of the Roman army. Years had passed since the city had been inhabited and the trinkets and coins had all been taken, but here was valuable stone. Already cut and dressed by master masons, it was easier to stack carts and sleds and barges with the good stone and send it wherever it was needed to continue to build the villas and temples and palaces of the Roman Empire than to go to the effort of quarrying it elsewhere and moving it long distances.

A small garrison of soldiers had been assigned to help assist engineers and masons in collecting the best stone and seeing it onto transports out of the area. Hard work for legionaries in the burning sun, but at least no one was trying to kill you.

One of their number was a mature man in his thirties called Jacobus. He'd joined the Roman army as a young man, at sixteen. He'd originally joined up with some youths from his village, not that they liked each other. Their officers had seen the bullying from the other recruits he'd joined up with, but initially ignored it, thinking of it as character building and that it would sort the wheat from the chaff, when it came to soldiers. However, when his intellect and expertise in mathematics was realised, Jacobus was quickly taken out of the front line and put to work on artillery engines, maintaining and firing the catapultum and ballista – the bolt and stone throwing machines – and using them to devastating effect in the field, against armies or in a siege. Jacobus rose quickly through the ranks, increasingly distancing himself from battle, retraining as an *Archetecti*, part of the *Milites Immunes* – individuals attached to the military, but possessing specialist skills that excused them from active combat, as an asset too valuable to waste being butchered by some barbarian. By the time he was sent to Carthage with a Centurion and one hundred men, Jacobus had been promoted to the position of *Optio Fabricae*, a high-ranking officer working alongside a Centurion and the men under his command.

His comrades from home, however, were not so lucky. History does not remember their names, as they became part of an ill-fated Legion that disappeared without trace in the depths of Western Europe and their records were lost over time. It was almost as if they had been scrubbed from History itself.

Now among the ruins of Carthage, Jacobus now had a task to deal with before the stone could be loaded and transported. The easiest point of access to the ruins that were of interest was over land, but a river stood in the way. It wasn't a very large river and the unit of legionaries and engineers constructed some rafts and transported themselves and their equipment, while men swam across with the animals, but it wasn't going to be possible to take stone backwards and forwards, so a bridge needed to be made.

There was plenty of building resources available so, after some preliminary investigations, a plan was made and materials brought to river's edge. The first order of work was to construct scaffolding across the river, so that construction could be carried out, into midstream from the water's edge. It was a gruelling, long, hot day, but at the end a framework stretching just over half way was built and the men washed and cooled off in the water as the sunset gave diamond tips to the little waves. Satisfied with their work, the men ate their evening meal back at their camp and drifted into a satisfied sleep.

* * *

Jacobus was woken by shouts of alarm and left his tent to hear garbled reports of the bridge scaffolding being found destroyed. Following the legionary who had brought the message back from dawn patrol back to the river, he found that the reports were indeed correct: The scaffolding had been broken up; but by who or what?

The soldiers said it must be locals, still angry and the Roman destruction of the city of Carthage, but when Jacobus inspected the wooden scaffolding poles, each as thick as a man's calf, some had been snapped in two and that was more than any man could accomplish. He'd seen elephants in the circuses and parades and had heard of their terrible strength when used in battle, but looking around there were no footprints, and elephants were hard to hide.

A search was conducted and some of the more 'persuasive' legionaries visited the locals to shake them down, but all came back with the same answer that no one seemed to know anything about the vandalism, so there was nothing to do but build the scaffolding again and leave a guard overnight.

* * *

It was another long, hard day for the men, working under the relentless North African sun, but again, by sundown half the river had been spanned with a wooden scaffold, ready for stone foundations to be laid the following day and a guard of six armed and armoured legionaries were left to stand guard against any potential vandals and that was that.

The sun set and the men washed and bathed, but without the same abandon as the previous night and there was a listlessness among the soldiers and the engineers as they retired to sleep.

* * *

It was deep in the night that the quiet was broken by the shouts of one of the guards and men started spilling form their tents, soldiers grabbing arms and shields and even the engineers laying their hands on mattocks and hammers, ready to repel vandals and insurgents. But the guard who'd run back to the camp wasn't shouting about men or weapons or assailant of any kind. No, he was raving about men made of rock, and dust devils – wind storms that whipped the sand into spirals – both tearing the wooden scaffolding apart, snapping logs, like twigs, and throwing great beams around like hazel wands.

By the time the sleep-roused camp arrived at the river, they found only the other five legionaries cowering behind and even under their shields, the scaffolding smashed to splinters and no amount of questioning or cajoling by their officers could get anything more sensible from them other than an explanation that the desert itself rose up, from either side of the river and destroyed the structure.

The next day, while the scaffold was built yet again and a new posting of ten legionaries with their *Decanus* officer was left to man the structure, the six guards from the night before were punished for failing in their duty and deserting their posts. Luckily the time it would take to send for new men meant they avoided execution and instead they were subjected to the less fatal, but far more agonising punishment of *bastinado*, where the soles of their feet were caned until they bled and then, with brutally injured feet they were put back on duty, carrying rock, hobbling back and forth, under threat of further punishment if they cried out or shied from their tasks, despite their sandals sopping wet with their own blood.

That night, Jacobus decided to stay with the guards and see for himself what was occurring and who was attacking their work. Borrowing armour, helm, shield and a short, legionary's *gladius* sword from the armoury, Jacobus took his shifts with the other men, watching nervously over the skeleton bridge, waiting to see who – or what – would come out of the desert.

* * *

The landscape turned from a sunset of dusty reds to a brilliantly pinpricked, starlit, silent black. The soldiers drew their cloaks close around them as the moon rose on the chilled darkness of the open horizon, throwing stark shadows where ancient stone lay tumbled in the unforgiving sand, and the river flowed on by with almost no sound and certainly no care for the men or what they were about to witness.

While the white disc of the moon reached it's zenith and the desert night found its coldest time as the heat of the day floated up and away into the cloudless star-filled sky, a breeze began to blow.

To begin with, none of the men noticed – it was just a night breeze – but as a deep rumble was heard, sounding like it came from the depths of the earth this startled the nodding soldiers and they came suddenly too wakefulness as the breeze grew stronger, tugging at cloaks and tunics.

Again, a loud rumble from beneath the ground was heard and this time it was clear that it came from the other side of the river and, looking across, Jacobus and the frightened men saw an explosion from the sand on the other bank. As they watched the sand settle it formed into a shape like the torso of a man, wading waist deep through the desert itself, with flailing arms and a head that flowed straight onto the shoulders. Where its face should have been a mouth yawned open and a roaring rumble poured from the mis-shapen hole as eyes of fire opened above it and glared at the huddled group across the river.

At the same time, on this side of the river, the wind quickly gathered speed, tightening and spinning into a miniature whirlwind – a dust devil – but like the monster on the other bank, it whipped the sand into an almost human shape, itself with a yawning, howling mouth and blazing, infernal eyes.

The men clustered together in the terrifying gale, their officer, the *Decanus* trying to bellow commands above the cacophony to bring his men into a formation, into some semblance of discipline and they locked their shields together and slowly retreated away from the dust whirling sand.

Unable to perform any useful action short of running away, Jacobus and the men watched as the two elemental beings roared and howled at each other across the river, almost thinking they could hear words among the tempest. Then the being of sand on the opposite bank plunged its great lumpen fist into the ground and pulled a huge rock out of the sand, like someone picking up a pebble from under water. Ponderously it leaned and twisted, then swung its arm up and over, flinging the rock like siege engine might throw a boulder, and the missile smashed into the wooden scaffolding, shattering and scattering the frame like reeds in the wind, sending poles, three times the height of a man, pin wheeling end over end towards the cowering legionaries.

At the last moment the Decanus screamed the order *Testudo!* and instinctively the men, Jacobus too, huddled in the middle of the group, responded to years of military training. The soldiers around the outside locked their shields together tightly while the men in the centre brought theirs up an over their heads, creating a protective cover like the shell of a tortoise, as the beams bounced off, leaving only painful bruises, rather than broken bones and split skulls.

From within their protective formation the men peeped between their shields and watched as now the dust devil howled and spun and tore at the scaffolding, while huge rocks rained down and waves of sand crashed at the structure until it was utterly rent apart.

Then suddenly, like the blowing out of a candle, the forms vanished, sand drifting back onto the ground, leaving no sign that either elemental had been there, and night returned to a chilled and empty silence.

After sufficient time had passed where it was felt that the desert elementals had definitely gone, the formation was relaxed and Jacobus went to survey the damage: Total destruction. None of the poles that had been painstakingly rigged and bound in position in the baking sun of the desert day were attached any more and most of beams that had been used had been snapped or smashed, leaving nothing standing.

* * *

The report to the camp leader, the Centurion, was a difficult one for Jacobus and the Decanus to give, but that they – and the other men – corroborated its extraordinary nature, meant he had to accept what he'd been told – and this was cold comfort to the six men who had been punished the day before.

A brief inspection of the site only confirmed this and all were at a loss as to what to do. Clearly, spending another day building yet another scaffolding only to have it smashed by these spirits of the desert was only going to invite destruction so, after day break, the officers of the camp busied their men with tasks, collecting, moving and stacking stone ready for transport while Jacobus and their other superiors debated on the next course of action.

It was part way through the afternoon, during a loud and heated argument declaring the various merits of relocating the bridge building area up or down stream that a guard announced a visitor to the camp – a Princess of a nomadic desert people, was asking to speak to the person in charge.

Under strict instructions to observe local customs as much as was possible, the Centurion invited the Princess into the main tent. Preceded by her guards – two huge men, built like oxen and with four-foot curved scimitars resting on their shoulders, the most beautiful and exotic looking woman Jacobus had ever seen entered the command tent: She was dressed in the traditional clothing of one of the Kabyle people, swathed in colourful fabrics, her heart-shaped face was composed and confident, but there was a smile behind her dark, almond eyes. Her skin was like burnished copper and her raven-black hair was braided and plaited in intricate designs, under a headdress made from silver coins, pierced and hung in strands almost as thick as ropes, showing her importance and the wealth of her family.

She smiled secretly and knowingly at Jacobus, which confused him somewhat, before inclining her head to the Centurion, who was clearly the most senior Roman present, and he invited her to sit and had wine and brought for her.

Being a military man and not a diplomat, the Centurion, anxious to avoid starting any unnecessary and messy troubles with local tribes, flustered and barked orders to bring him a translator, but the words died in his throat as the Princess introduced herself in perfect, but deliciously accented Latin.

She told the Centurion that her name was Fazluna and that her people lived and moved through the great desert wastes of what we now know as North Africa and that she was a Princess among her folk. She told the assembled men that she was also a seer, blessed with the power to see into the future, the past and the present; she said that she had dreamt of the men she looked at now and how they were plagued by destructive forces and that she knew what was needed to help.

After the report from the previous night and the evidence of its truth, the Centurion invited her to tell them what she knew, and as cool Roman wine was poured, quenching the parched sandy throats of the listening men, Fazluna told a story of two brothers…

> In the time before the great city state of Carthage, when the desert was a howling wasteland, where only the Kabyle dared to live, moving from oasis to oasis, sheltering from the burning sun beneath their richly decorated tents and awnings, and dining on milk and dates and fish from the scant pools and hidden valleys that dotted the wastes, there was a great and powerful spirit, of fire and air, one of the Djinns of the deserts.
>
> When the people came to build the city of Carthage they bargained with the Djinn who allowed them to build their clumsy and immovable buildings of stone and even tore rock from deep beneath the desert sands to give to them, so that they could cut it to shape and

use it in their dwellings and fortifications and in return, certain hidden temples were built beneath the city where he was honoured and offerings given – the most important of which housed a rare and precious gem known as the Fire Jewel: A deep red ruby, with fire in its heart and the Djinn was proud of this jewel that had been dedicated to him.

In time, this Djinn had two sons who were, like him, spirits of the desert and the three of them would, from time to time, appear before the priests who venerated them and grant favours or counsel wisdom.

But the memories of men are short and as the years passed fewer and fewer offerings were made, and more and more of the temples were turned over to the new Gods of Carthage and the Djinn and his sons were forgotten.

But even though the men had forgotten him, *he* did not forget the first pacts that had been made and honoured them. When the Romans first came and attacked the city, the Djinn and his two sons stood ready on a distant hill, wreathed in fire, clad in white hot armour and armed with swords whose waving, serpentine blades were licked with tongues of blue flame, waiting for the call to defend Carthage.

Forgotten they stood, uncalled, glorious in their blazing manifestation, and watched as building by building, wall by wall, stone by stone, the great city, its inhabitants haemorrhaging into the inhospitable desert, was pulled to the ground by the mighty Legions of Rome.

It is said that as he watched the destruction, tears of fire ran down the Djinn's face and little by little, as the city disintegrated, so his essence, in sorrow and despair, blew away on the desert wind until there was nothing left of him and the brothers were left fatherless.

In their grief, they assumed human form and descended on the ruins, trying to find the Fire Jewel that had been dedicated to their Father. Splitting up to search, the ruined city, they each delved among the rubble and the hidden passages until they found the old temples. One brother finally found the place where the Fire Jewel had rested, but finding it gone and encountering a thief who was scavenging the destruction he grabbed the man by the throat, lifting him off the ground with fire pouring from his eyes, unable to hide his true form, demanding to know where was the stone that rightfully belonged to him and his brother.

Now, in truth, the thief did not know the whereabouts of the jewel, but understood that the truth was unlikely to satisfy the incandescent spirit, and so told the Djinn that his brother had already been there and taken it.

Releasing the unfortunate man and flying to his brother with feelings of joy he asked him where their jewel was, but, of course, the other denied possessing it and the two brothers fell to arguing about how the other must already have it, and had taken it for themselves.

Blinded by grief and tangled amongst the thorns of mistrust the brothers returned to the desert, each declaring their home on either side of a river and that neither would cross nor allow the other to cross until the one who had stolen the jewel returned it to the other, for both to devote to their Father's memory.

There was silence in the tent as she finished her story and sat back in her chair, her sharp eyes expectantly looked from man to man, sipping the cool, golden wine.

Jacobus and the Centurion looked at each other, confused.

Fazluna sighed at their lack of comprehension and so pointed out of the tent towards where the bridge was supposed to be being made. "That river", she explained and light dawned on the men's faces.

"Very well", said the Centurion, a practical man. "So we need to find another place to build a bridge."

"You could do", replied Fazluna. "But the land the brothers claim as theirs extends far up and down stream and what use would that be?"

"What do you suggest?" asked Jacobus.

"That you return the jewel and stop the brothers from fighting", Fazluna answered.

As the men were about to ask how his feat was to be achieved, smiling mischievously over her goblet, the young woman pulled up one of her necklaces, a large and decorative pendant appearing from the folds of her silks. It was circular with gold and amber beads radiating from the centre, like the rays of the sun, or flames of a fire. At the central point of radiation there was a single, deep-red jewel.

"The ruby?"

The young woman nodded. "And I am prepared to exchange this, and tell you how *you*", she pointed at Jacobus, "will be able to deliver it to the brothers, in return for certain privileges, allowances of free passage and protection by the Roman Empire for my people".

The two men exchanged glances.

"It is, after all", Fazluna continued, "Simply wasteland and has no intrinsic value, except as a crossing point. My tribe will be allowed to pass freely over the bridge and to extract a toll to all non-Roman travellers, in return for maintaining and protecting the bridge, once your work here is done: My people will control the crossing – in the name of the Roman Empire, naturally. I will set up a camp on the other bank with my attendants to oversee this".

The Centurion flustered. "You? Wouldn't a man – your father, a brother, or cousin – be better?"

"Amongst *my* people", bridled the Princess, "Women have as much to say as men – we measure a person's value by their ability and not by what is between their legs".

The Centurion flushed a deep red, and reminded himself of the directive to observe local traditions and customs, but Jacobus smirked at the young woman's frankness and hid an appreciative grin in his cup. Fazluna was truly the most unusual and wonderful woman he'd met.

In the awkward silence, after composing himself, Jacobus sat up in his seat, cleared his throat and asked, "Why me?"

Fazluna turned her dark eyes on the man, smiled, and answered, "Because I have seen it. I know you, as we have met many times in my dreams. I know it is you who must do this and I know how you will accomplish it". And that was all she would say on the matter.

* * *

After the meeting, the men discussed the transaction and agreed it would be a small price to pay as the land, as the Princess said, was essentially wilderness anyway and that, if she could accomplish what she claimed and tame the ravaging desert spirits, then they could get on with their job and start getting the thousands of tonnes of stone prepared and transported, so they sent a messenger to Fazluna's camp and contracts were drawn up between scribes. When this had been done, the Princess sent for Jacobus to visit her tent, where she was to instruct him in what needed to be done, to placate the destructive Djinns.

* * *

Her nearby encampment was a magical place: Great tents, some cotton, some silk – all painted with rich designs and scenes from the stories of the Kabyle people. They billowed and waved in the warm afternoon breeze, while camels, in a corral chewed and bellowed, as he approached. Men, swathed in cloth against the desert sun, wind and sand, moved to and fro attending to various duties, while the same huge guards as had visited his camp stood sentinel in the shade of an awning, outside what was the most beautiful, most lavishly decorated and clearly the most important tent – that of the Princess Fazluna.

Inside, he and the Princess were conspicuously alone together. Lounging on large, soft cushions, in the shady interior, with braziers burning strongly fragrant incense, she poured a thick, sweet, strong drink with a name Jacobus couldn't pronounce. She told him it was produced from dates and should be drunk in small measurers; this last point he noted as Fazluna poured two large cups of the sticky liquid.

"In my dreams", the Princess began, "I not only saw the Djinn brothers and how they raised the desert against you and destroyed your building work, but I also saw how you presented them with the Fire Jewel, reconciling their brotherhood and allowing you to build your little bridge. I had an artisan draw this from my descriptions".

She rolled out a parchment on a low table next to where she was reclining and beckoned Jacobus over to sit next to her, to inspect it. Even with the smoking incense he could smell her strong perfume and made an effort to concentrate on the task in hand and remember that she was a Princess and he, an Optio Fabricae – a servant of the Roman Empire.

It was a drawing of a very simple pillar of stacked stones, with a hole, bored from top to bottom. The Princess, after refilling Jacobus' cup again with the strong, sweet drink, went to explain that he was supposed to build this midstream, to form the central supporting pillar of his bridge in one day and then, at midnight, to call upon the brothers, with the Fire Jewel in his hands, and that this had to be accomplished in a single day, before midnight.

Despite the intoxicating atmosphere and his strong awareness of the closeness of this equally intoxicating and, for a Roman man, unusually independent woman, Jacobus reviewed the drawing and listened to Fazluna's instructions on the execution of the task and thought it all seemed achievable.

"Good", she said, letting the parchment spring back into its original rolled up state and turning to look at Jacobus, her face only inches from his. "Now, let me tell you of something of the customs of my people".

The rest of the afternoon was spent 'improving diplomatic relations'.

At sunset Jacobus returned to his own camp where the Centurion, smelling incense and perfume on top of the drink on his Optio's breath, was mollified by the drawings from Fazluna's artisan and her instructions, but simply scowled at Jacobus as he started to bluff and fluster, and stumble over his description of the rest of his meeting with the Princess, and growled, "I don't want to know".

* * *

The next day was spent in preparation: Stone was selected and cut, to make the pillar, and more beams were stacked, ready to make scaffolding that would reach midstream, but nothing was put in place – everything was made ready for one great effort the next day.

A peaceful night passed, with no visitation from the Djinns, as nothing had been built, so there was nothing to destroy. In the hour before dawn the Roman legionaries and engineers, supervised by Jacobus and the Centurion, and watched over by Princess Fazluna and her entourage, waited by the water's edge. They stood, looking to the eastern horizon, the silence broken only by the sound of the tents flapping in an early breeze.

The horizon lightened, fading from black to a dark purple, to deep blue, to red until, like a Fire Jewel itself, the top of the rising sun broke the horizon, signalling the start of a new day. As soon as this happened the Centurion roared out an order which was echoed by the voices of the Decani, calling their men to action and swiftly the wood was taken to the water's edge and construction began in earnest.

The building continued apace all day with shifts of men working under the cruel desert sun, lashing the wooden beams together, slowly reaching further and further across the river. By late afternoon rafts were launched onto the water, carrying the great, heavy blocks of stone, that were to make the central pillar, described in Fazluna's drawings. Ropes already wrapped around the huge blocks were attached to cranes, hurriedly built on the wooden scaffold, and the stones lifted and swung, using counterweights and pivots, slowly lowered into the water and gently settled on the riverbed at the precise middle point of the crossing. A hole had been bore through all the stones, so as the first was lowered into place a very long, thin pole was put into that stone's centre so the others could be placed accurately on top, like a child's game of stacking rings.

The sun had set hours before the last stone was put in place, the men working by the light of flaming torches, flickering and guttering in the desert winds. Now for the final part, as Jacobus, Fire Jewel in hand was ferried out to stand on top of the stone pillar, midstream, a torch in one hand and the rafts brought ashore and the scaffolding hurriedly dismantled within the hour.

Everything that had been constructed was now deconstructed, with only the pillar remaining, rising from the very centre of the river, with Jacobus, standing atop it, like the statue of a hero.

Time passed, the stars rolled across the sky and a full moon rose when the midnight hour arrived.

As that time arrived so a wind picked up, turning small eddies and twists, lifting the sand. From the opposite shore a low rumbling was heard from deep in the ground and suddenly the desert rose on each side – one a twisting, howling dust devil of viciously spiralling sand, the other a rough man shape of flowing sand and both approached the river from their sides. The Romans and the Kabyle watched from a distance, as the two elemental forms of the Djinns crashed down to the river, but both appeared confused, hesitating, as there was nothing easily reachable that was clearly coming from or going to the other side. This was Jacobus' moment and he held the Fire Jewel high in the air, the flickering flame of the torch making it sparkle red, just as the sun had done at the dawn of that day.

"Mighty Djinns!" he cried. "I have found your Father's jewel and I hold it here in my hand! Listen to me or I shall cast it into the waters of the river to be lost forever!"

At this, the elemental forms the Djinns had taken fell away, the sand dropping to the ground and from the clouds of falling sand two figures stepped into the night and walked towards the riverbanks. Each figure was human in shape, but their skin shone and reflected the torchlight as if they were made of solid gold, glinting and sparking in the moonlight, and their eyes glowed and flared, like flaming coals.

"Give it to me!" bellowed one of the golden Djinns, stretching out his hand and continuing to walk forward, stepping onto the surface of the water as if it was as solid as a paved floor.

"No!" ordered the other, also stepping onto the river's surface and stretching out his hand. "Give it to *me*!"

"Come no closer!" cried Jacobus, holding the jewel over the ripping surface. "You may be able to walk this river like a road, but the jewel will sink into its depths and be carried away if you come any closer", and both the shining, flame-eyed Djinns stopped, looking between each other and Jacobus.

"What do you want for it?" asked one of the brothers.

"I will give you gold", said the other, coins pouring from his hands and splashing into the dark waters of the river.

"I will give you jewels", said the second, making emeralds, diamonds and sapphires rain from the air around him, pitter-pattering on the river's surface as they fell like rain onto and into the water.

"I will give you palaces and power", now said the first, pointing behind him as a vast palace rose from the ground, sand pouring off it walls and minarets, the moonlight shining on its white walls.

"What I want", called Jacobus, interrupting the second Djinn as he was about to make an even greater offer, and realising quite how much these two were willing to give for the one jewel and trying to ignore the part of himself that was suggesting it might be a good idea to take one of them up on their offers. "What I want", he started again, "is for the two of you to remember why you prize this jewel so highly: That this was your Father's jewel and as his sons this reminds you of him and both of you want it equally as much, but you have forgotten that as well as being your Father's sons you are also brothers and your desire to posses this jewel has clouded your love for each other and besmirched your Father's memory."

The golden Djinns stared at each other across the river, their flaming eyes unreadable.

"What I want is to build a bridge here and for you to watch over it and the people who will protect it. In return I will make this fire jewel part of the bridge itself, to honour your Father's memory".

Silence.

Standing on top of the pillar midstream, Jacobus looked from one fiery metallic figure to the other as they stood on the water's surface, looking impassively at each other, the pillar between them.

Seconds ticked by until one of the Djinns spoke, over the water to his brother, "This mortal is right. We have forgotten that we are brothers."

"In our grief we have forgotten our Father and forgotten why we wanted this jewel", replied the other.

"I am willing to agree to his suggestions if you are", said the first.

"As am I", replied his brother and both looked to Jacobus and nodded their agreement.

Holding the Fire Jewel up high, for both brothers and the distant group of people to see, he let the light of the flickering torch play on it, rousing the fire in it's bloody depths and then slowly bent down, so the brothers could see what he was doing and dropped the gemstone into the hole that had been bored down through the centre of the pillar.

Seeing this done, one of the Djinns turned and walked back to the shore, before turning to face his brother across the water. Then, with slow deliberation the spirit lifted one foot and placed it in front of him and, as he did so, stone appeared out the air, growing and expanding. With each step he took forward, more stone appeared and a bridge magically began to form beneath his feet. Taking the lead from his brother, the other Djinn started to walk and create the other side of the bridge. As the brothers approached and the bridge came towards a point, Jacobus leapt from his pillar into the water and struck out for the bank. The two brothers met at the apex, supported by the column Jacobus had built, and embraced each other.

As the assembled Romans and Kabyle watched, the two Djinns, holding each other close, began to dull in colour, the sparkle leaving their metallic skins until they became the colour of the desert sand and began to blow away in the breeze until, finally, no trace of them remained upon the magically created bridge and the desert night returned to its cold, starry silence.

* * *

From that moment on, the two brothers were never seen again by mortal eyes – at least none who had the courage to report it – and, while the bridge itself eventually weathered away and was replaced with more modern materials and to suite more modern traffic, as the centuries passed, the pillar, still containing the hidden Fire Jewel remained, and remains to this day as a mark of unification and of the story of the two Djinn brothers, and woe betide any who topple the pillar or cause the Fire Jewel to be lost in the waters of the river.

It is only left to say that Jacobus remained in the area to oversee the ongoing salvage of the Carthaginian masonry and continued to improve 'diplomatic relations' with the Kabyle people – with one Kabyle person in particular. At the end of his remaining tenure in the army of Rome, he chose to stay, and married his Princess and their children went on to have many adventures of their own.

Child of the Seasons Part 1 (Winter Ice), Montesquieu-Avantès, France

Winter was cold.

It's always cold.

It's meant to be cold, so the old year can die and a new year can be born – but that year, especially this far south in France it was a particularly cold winter.

It was so cold the few leaves left clinging to the trees snapped off if you brushed by them.

It was so cold that if a man were outside, working the fields, his moustaches would turn to icicles, drooping from his face.

It was so cold that pebbles on the riverbanks froze together and what was once moving shingle became a pavement of solid stone.

It was cold in the fields, it was cold in the homes, but, for Madeleine, it was also cold in her heart as, with mattocks to break open the solid ground, the people of her village helped bury her mother, her last remaining relative, and she returned to a lonely house, empty of people. The only company she now had were the few goats she and her mother had kept for milk and occasional meat; they had been brought inside the one-room wood and thatch building, to protect them from the cold, and provide a little additional warmth for the house's final residents – animals and women sleeping close to the central fire, at night.

The house hadn't always been so empty.

Growing up at the edge of the village, on the edge of the forest, there had once been the warm, familial hustle and bustle of her mother and father and her two brothers. As infants, the older boys did household chores, while her parents spun flax and wove linen, her mother's sharp eyes and nimble fingers adding delicate borders of embroidery in bright threads of reds and blues and yellows and greens that she found so fascinating as a little girl. As she had got older she had helped out more around the house, fetching and carrying and cleaning; then learning to spin; next learning her mother's skill at needlework in an atmosphere of love and laughter.

But as the years passed, the house had become quieter and colder. Her father slipped away, taken by an illness that swiftly crept through his body in a matter of weeks. The younger of her brothers, still a boy at the time, had been kicked by a horse and pronounced '*dead before he hit the ground*'. Her older brother had gone to war and stayed there, as many young men did … and still do. Madeleine carried on, because that is what you do, and some years passed before she woke to find that her mother, her last remaining relative in the whole of the world, had passed away quickly and quietly in her sleep, and now Madeleine was alone.

But Madeleine shouldn't have been alone. As was the custom for the people in her village and those nearby, she should have been married some years by now.

But Madeleine was born different.

When she was born, the features and structures of her face were not like other people's.

Today we understand that disfigurement is something that can happen during a child's development, before birth, but in pre-medieval, rural France, where superstition ran rampant and religion was enforced with the fear of punishment in this life and the next, there were many who thought her features were the sign of something much darker, and all her life she had heard other villagers whisper that she had been sired by the devil, an abomination who was likely his servant – a witch. Whenever outside her house, even in her own garden, Madeleine would wear a scarf to hide a face that anyone except her family turned away from.

No one came home with her after the burial to comfort her in her grief. Only Madame Pecheux, who served as the local midwife and had helped bring her into the world, offered her any comfort and solace as she left the frost-bitten graveyard; the vibrant threads of her childhood gone and replaced by a drab void. So now, alone, at the edge of the village, at the edge of the forest and doomed to decline in solitude and persecution, Madeleine decided instead to set her goats free, leave her home and walk into the frozen forest.

Still wearing her best clothes from the funeral – hardly the right clothes for the weather – she walked despondently away from the house she'd grown up in. The snow melted on her smart, soft shoes, soaking through the thin leather and the feet of her stockings, and quickly the chilled, sodden footwear started to freeze and pain slowly turned to a blessed numbing.

Deep in the forest and deep in despair, she came across a place where she and her brothers had played as children. It was a quiet place: Far from people, and silent under the covers of winter snow, the trees were bare, rheumatic fingers pointing up towards an unforgiving deep grey, pregnant sky.

In front of her was a wide, flat circle of virgin snow that she knew covered a deep pool. In the summer it was clear, refreshing to drink and peopled with thrumming dragonflies and the occasional stilt-walking heron. Now, it was quiet in winter's cold sleep.

Picking up a sturdy fallen branch she stepped out confidently, feeling the thick ice beneath her feet, hearing it creak and groan as she walked purposefully, towards the centre.

Standing in the middle of the pool's icy surface she cast her eyes about, looking for a reason, for something to change her mind, but finding nothing she raised the branch, like a giant pestle and brought the butt of the stave down, hard, on the ice at her feet.

There was a deep boom as the force of the blow echoed through the frozen water, and the snow covering the ice bounced for a moment, and then silence and stillness again.

She lifted the branch and again brought it down, even harder, between her feet: another deep boom and creaking, but then stillness again.

As she lifted the wood for the third time a sudden whining creak turned into a crack, like a whip, and the ice opened beneath her.

Deep she fell, her skirts and petticoats enveloping her, swaddling her, but the shock of the sudden and complete immersion in freezing water drove the breath from her body and she began to sink, stunned and breathless to the bottom of the pool. Above her, the icy ceiling glowed blue, the thin winter sun lighting it from behind as she drifted down, down to lie in the soft mud, submerged, frozen, and hidden from the world that had turned its back on her.

Coming to rest in the silt, the blue ice above her dimming as her vision darkened, Madeleine was unaware of what else lay in the cold bed, around and beneath her.

Long ago, long before the name of Christ had been brought from far away, long before the Romans, long, even, before the Celtic tribes, people had lived and farmed and, more importantly, worshipped in this land. Beneath the young woman's body was layer upon layer of coins, bracelets, arm rings, swords, cups, statues, necklaces, beads and other valuable votive pieces, suspended in the soft mud – offerings hidden in the dark, there to please the gods and spirits.

The people who had worshipped here had indeed pleased their gods with their offerings and those gods had not forgotten. As Madeleine's salt tears mingled freely with the sweet water of the icy forest pool, and as *her* heart slowed, another's woke.

Deep from his sleep, deep from the depths of the pool and deep from the slumbering sap in the trees; deep from the loamy earth and deep from the hearts of stag and boar and wolf, an ancient mind woke and heard the sadness in the young woman's fading heart, as one sees the dying embers in the ashes of a fire, and he caught her as she fell, and held her between the worlds.

As she dangled between life and death Madeleine opened her eyes and in the spinning gloom she beheld something that was both man and animal. He stood, naked, on two legs, but had a short, flicking tail, great antlers sprouted from his head and his eyes were imponderable, dizzying pools, and she was content to stay, somehow, both lying in his arms and hanging in the nothingness, in front of his deeply masculine, bestial form. When he spoke, he spoke directly, deeply into her soul and offered her a choice: the choice to continue her fall to the lands of the dead or to return to the lands of the living, as his bride.

"But I am not beautiful enough for such a thing as you. I am not beautiful enough to be any sort of bride. I am not beautiful at all", she said, reaching out to stroke its feral features and at the same time touching her own face.

"I measure beauty in life and not in shape", replied the spirit. "The bark of a tree may grow this way or that, but it is the tree as a whole that is of interest. If a rock is cleft there within may grow a fern, or when the clouds are rent by the wind to shape and reshape time and again, therein I see their beauty".

And Madeleine felt the spirit's sincerity and warmth and power, and allowed herself to sink into his arms, and the darkness enveloped her entirely.

* * *

When she woke, all Madeleine could see was white.

She was lying on her side and snow was piled up in front of her, as if she had been pushed along the ground. Twisting to look behind her she saw the frozen pool, and sitting up, she saw the hole in the centre where she had fallen through, and then the hole at the edge where the ice had been smashed and she had clearly been dragged up and out.

There were no footprints, no signs of anyone having been there, except her. The only strange thing was how exposed the roots of the trees were at the edge of the water where she'd been pulled out, as if they had burst up out of the ground and later sought to wriggle back under the earth.

Standing up, she became aware of just how sodden her clothing was, but instead of feeling the cold she held up her arms to look at the steam that was rising from her body: An inner heat warmed her and every step she took towards home, her footprints melted the snow and left dark patches on the bare earth.

Reaching her house, she lit a fire and changed out of her damp, muddied clothes. It was then she noticed two things: Firstly, a gold bracelet of exquisite craftsmanship on her left wrist; not only was it beautiful, it was also too small to have passed over her hand; but it was there.

The second thing she noticed was a change in herself, and the knowledge that new life was growing inside her.

* * *

Jacques was born in the spring.

No one in the village thought it odd that Madeleine had become pregnant and no one questioned the very brief period of her pregnancy. When her labour pains came, Madame Pecheux heard her cries and came to help bring her little one into the world as she did with all the mothers. While Madeleine rested, the midwife took the baby around the village to meet everyone. It wasn't the usual custom, but it seemed right this time, and the little newling met the village elders, the priest, the baker, the brewer and everyone else and all their families, and everyone loved him.

It was a peculiar thing, although few commented on it, but as he grew and the seasons changed, so did the colour of the boy's eyes, earning him the name *Jacques des Saisons*: In spring his eyes were the bright green of new shoots, of unfurling leaves, of fresh blades of grass; in the summer they were golden like the sun, like ripening corn; in autumn they dulled to a deep amber, like the leaves that fall from the trees and the sombre heads of forest mushrooms, and in winter … they were the colour of ice.

No one questioned how Madeleine's garden now grew with such abundance or where the ancient gold coins came from that she shared so generously with the church and the needy, but when, as the years passed and, as all things must, Madeleine slipped away from this world, the people were sad to see her go.

They were even more sad when, after his mother was laid in the ground next to her own parents and her brothers and, after speaking to the priest, saying how he was giving what was now his house and grounds to the church, for the use of the poor, Jacques des Saisons also left.

On a winter's day when the weather was particularly cold, he smiled his charming, bright smile, before leaving the sad, waving people and he headed off into the forest.

Woodwose, the Wild Woods of Central Europe [across borders]

B efore the crushing tribal tread,
Of conquering mankind came,
The world was forest from East to West,
Without fences, or borders, or name.

Then bighting axes cleaved great wounds,
That never could be healed,
Wielded, unthinking, by human hands,
First stone, then bronze and then steel.

And as the mighty titans fell,
To be butchered for hearth and home,
The little mortals who ravaged them,
Soon found they weren't alone.

For beneath the boughs and between shady trunks,
And green, sunlit dapplings,
As well as boar and bear and wolf,
Lived more ancient, magical things.

Some trees, themselves, got up and walked,
Squashing houses and people alike,
There were Leshy and Moosleute and Hinky Punks,
And mischievous, bright-eyed Sprites.

There were seductive Dryads, tree spirits who,
Would take away men who went without care,
And striding, thick-legged mushroom beings,
Who puffed deadly spores in the air.

These and many more were there,
Who were the woodsman's bane,
Until a Wildman, unknown, unthanked,
To save the forest folk, came.

The few who saw him gave him many a name,
Some real, some imagined we suppose,
Known as 'Jacques des Saison' or 'Jack in the Green',
Or just as the wild forest man – Woodwose.

He had hair like a shrub filled with creepers and nests,
And a beard to his waste to match,
It sprung from his head and it sprung from his chin,
Like an unkempt century-old thatch.

In the spring there'd be flowers sprouting out of his hair,
And his eyes were as green as the grass,
In the summer there'd be ears of corn in his beard,
And his eyes were like amber glass.

Come the autumn he'd bare fruit and mushrooms to boot,
His eyes brown, like two harvest mice.
But in the winter he'd be barren and gaunt like a bone,
And his eyes cold with death, like blue ice.

Those who met him all liked him, but thought him eccentric,
They said he was ever so odd,
But they saw only the half that was a man, like themselves,
Not the other half: part ancient God.

So he travelled the woods and the forested hills,
And danced to satyrs' flutes,
He'd walk on the ground or leap between branches,
Or sink into the earth among roots.

What the people did not know – for he did not show,
As they busied like bees in their hives,
Was the battle against darkness, against moss-covered dead,
Against goblins who came for their lives.

They'd try and take babies, asleep in their cots,
Or lure away children at play,
They seduced husbands and sometimes the wives,
Or simply attacked people at work, night and day.

Tirelessly he fought to preserve, what he thought
Of as the good heart of the woodlands, as well
As the villages, houses and hovels in which,
The people of the forest did dwell.

The magical part of him kept him alive,
Beyond any normal lifespan,
But eventually he was spent, and like all things he went,
Into the earth like a mortal man.

The good spirits of the woods found him a place,
Where none could disturb him or see,
So, quietly they buried him, down among roots,
And above him they grew a tree.

Through their magic protection and guardian spells,
The wood spirits hid him where he'd never be found,
So, unknown to those who he'd saved or he'd helped,
Among trees, the Woodwose slept in the ground.

If you go there today – if you knew the way,
There'd be nothing but woodland to see,
Only saplings and grasses and low forest flowers,
Blooming at the base of a tree.

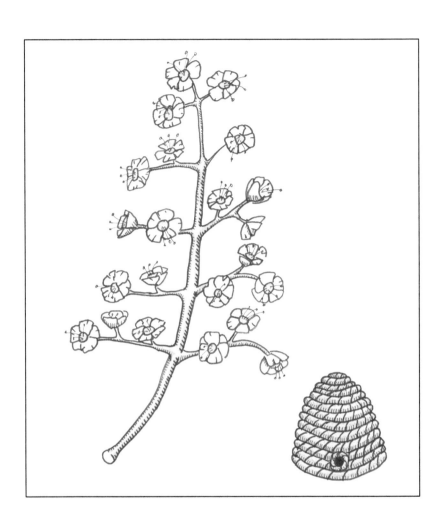

Child of the Seasons Part 2 (Spring Honey), Southern Bohemia [Czech Republic]

Let us start by discussing flowers and, in particular, the flowers of the horse chestnut tree *aesculus hippocastanum*. More famous for its seeds – the shiny brown conkers, surrounded by fleshy, green cases, bristling with spikes – the flowers of the horse chestnut are often too high for people to see closely when it comes into blossom in spring, especially as the lower branches are usually cropped bare by deer and forest-roaming cattle. But, when the tree does blossom it is a lofty giant, up to one hundred and twenty feet tall with conical clusters of flowers, or 'candles', studding the outer surfaces, at the ends of its branches.

Up close, each flower candle is comprised of a central vertical stalk, with laterally radiating smaller stalks, much like a child's drawing of a Christmas tree. The flowers are evenly spread along these smaller stalks, with clusters of small, flat, splayed white petals, splashed with pink and yellow, like hand-painted porcelain, and from the centres of the flowers a group of equally white filaments, rise, terminating in anthers – dusted yellow landing pads for insects, covered in pollen and offering promises of sweet nectar deep between the folds of the petals.

These paint-spattered blossoms are much loved by bees and, in the perfumed spring, the insects are welcomed by the seductive tree. After their tryst the bees fly away, their colourful, furry little bodies powder-puffed with pollen grains and in an intimate drowse from indulging in the nectar, move on to another petalled lover, ensuring the future generations of both bees and horse chestnut trees.

The gift of new life these jewelled little workers distribute across our lands, across our mortal boundaries and national borders is often forgotten in light of the sticky, sweet honey they make in their combs, to raise their broods.

Honey is miraculous: it has been used since time immemorial to dress wounds, killing off infections and speeding the healing process. It also seems to be incorruptible having been found laid down in ceremonial burial jars in tombs from over five thousand years ago. But it's the sticky, sweet taste that we love so much. Honey made by bees that have visited different flowers has differing tastes – some gentle and teasing, others rich and so strong it tingles the tongue almost to the point of burning.

In very ancient times people had to forage for honey, looking for tell-tale dark ribbons of bees flying to and from splits in the trunks of trees, or cave mouths, or holes in cliffs, before climbing to dangerous heights and braving attack from the enraged swarms defending their offspring and their queen from the ravages of the intruder.

But with honey as such a prize, as was done with the ferocious, tusked boar, the lethal juggernaut wild cattle, and the man-eating wolf, bees were domesticated and people tamed the stinging hordes and provided them with safe hives protected from the cold and the rain, and with access to nectar-rich flowers, in return for a share of their golden harvest.

* * *

Returning to the horse chestnut trees, with which we started, there is one in particular which is very important to our story and is a very important tree in its own right. Perhaps you know why it's important; Slavěna, who lived on her own, nearby, only knew it was important to her bees, to make their honey, but there was greater power in it than the young woman suspected, and we must remember this, as it will become evident later in our story.

In case you *don't* know how the tree came to be important I shall tell you.

There was once a man – or at least something like a man – born of a woman who, it was said, had married a god and consummated their bond beneath our world, in an in-between place where there is no life or death, no heaven or hell, and from this union he was conceived. He was born far away, but had travelled many lands and ended up in this little corner of Bohemia.

Some of the older folk in the village remembered threadbare stories about him: That his beard grew down to his knees and was woven with vines and leaves, and birds nested within it. It was said that in the spring his eyes were green, in the summer they were golden yellow, in autumn they were nut-brown and, in winter, ice-blue. He lived wild in the forest and had many names, including 'Jack of the Seasons' and, more locally, Zelený Honza – Green Jack.

This story is not about him, but its beginning is in his ending.

Any who knew the forest-man would have said he must have been at least in his seventies or even eighties – a venerable age – but what they didn't realise was that when he died, as all things must, his age was seven times seven, times seven, and if you do the calculations you will know that made him three hundred and forty three years old.

No one from the surrounding villages attended his funeral – they wouldn't have known where to find it – but the people who did know – *his* type of people – found a place in the forest that had meaning, dug a grave for him and laid him in it, surrounded by flowers and ferns. He was laid on his side, curled up, as if peacefully sleeping, and placed into his hands was a single, glossy, brown horse chestnut conker, and then the grave was covered and hidden by the sowing of grass and wild flower seeds.

Nearly half a century later, the green man's grave was nowhere to be seen and on its site stood a mighty tree, with large teardrop-shaped leaves in groups of fives and sevens, with conkers in the autumn and, naturally, flowers in the spring.

It was in late spring one year, on a rose-dusted afternoon, that Slavěna was checking her hives. They were made from straw, twisted into rope-like coils, that were stitched together as they wound up in decreasing circles, and she had placed them far enough from her house to avoid attracting new colonies moving in, under the thatched eaves of her home, but close enough to be convenient and safe. All seemed to be in order: there was a steady column of bees returning home, ready for the night, and no bears had wrecked any of the domed hives, in their insatiable search for honey, so she returned to her house and her patient.

Normally, Slavěna lived alone, having taken on a cottage that others in the nearby village thought unlucky for lost reasons that whispered echoes of something to do with the big tree, not a native of the area – but what possible power could a tree have?

Slavěna didn't follow the traditions, customs and superstitions of her neighbours. Even her parents despaired of her – why hadn't she wanted to get married? Why couldn't she be like the other girls? She should realise that men knew better than women and she should know her place.

Avoiding the womanly roles of traditional life, she was, however, much respected for the honey her bees made and, particularly by the landlord of the local tavern among others, for her medovina – the strong, sweet, honey wine, we know in English as mead.

In fact, it had been on her way back from dropping a delivery of medovina at the local tavern – the sign of the Green Man – that she had met her patient: Although she didn't normally get involved with other people's conflicts, stepping out of the tavern onto the sunny street, a drunken brute was manhandling a slight-figured woman, about the same age as herself and half the size of her attacker. He held her painfully tight by the wrist as she pulled and pleaded with him and he raged and shook her, bellowing, slurring at her. The woman he held was crying, apologising and pleading, her tears making blood from a cut under one eye run down her cheek, like the sanguine weeping of a miraculous statue.

Inflamed by the sight of someone being bullied so viciously and seeing no one coming to the woman's assistance, without a thought for her own safety, she strode over, her arms pumping the air and her jaw set grimly.

"Leave her alone, you fat-headed bullock!" she cried, pulling the man by one shoulder, making him spin on the spot, reeling unsteadily in his stupor. He blearily focussed his pink, drink-pouched eyes on her, squinting through the alcoholic fog.

"Oh!" he cried in mock surprise and released the woman he'd been beating, so suddenly she stumbled and fell in the dust, adding to her scrapes and bruises. "The Queen Bee spinster comes to give me orders!" he made a mocking bow, stumbling and shuffling to stop himself falling over.

"Why don't you bring me a few bottles of your medovina and we'll see if you stay barren for long", he growled, leering and reaching out for her. Batting the drunkard's arm aside and ignoring him, Slavěna stooped to help the other woman, who was rising painfully from the ground.

"What's your name?" asked Slavěna, kindly, looking into the deep brown of the woman's tear-pooled eyes.

"Dana – Bogdana – but people call me Dana", muttered the woman between sobs, wincing as she stood.

"Right, Dana", said Slavĕna, looking intently into the other woman's face. "You're coming with me. I'll fix you up and you'll feel a lot better afterwards".

Dana said nothing, sniffing and hobbling, trying to keep her weight off what was clearly a painful leg.

"You'll do nothing of the sort", roared the drunkard. "She is my wife! – worse luck for me – and it is my right, as her husband, to treat her as I see fit, and I see fit to punish her for her nagging and scolding and laziness".

"Your wife!" Slavĕna was dumfounded. She thought that the unfortunate Dana had been accosted by a drunk in the street and not realised that she was actually married to this bloodshot, sweating pig.

"Yes!" sneered the man. "And you will keep your spinster's nose out of my marriage", and shoved Slavĕna full in the chest, his strength and weight making her stagger back and almost losing her balance, but she was back and straight at him, and slapped him full in the face. His response was swift and brutal, swinging his arm up and wide, hitting the back of his fist against the side of her head.

The world slowed and Slavĕna felt herself take a few heavy plods backwards and then her legs turned to water, her knees buckled and she sat down hard, on the ground, unsure of what was happening or who she was.

By the time her head cleared she became aware that the landlord and a number of his patrons had spilled out of the tavern and were now sitting on the writhing, thrashing drunkard who was shouting threats and curses at the men, at his wife, at Slavĕna and at the world in general. The two women helped each other up and, with an understanding nod from the landlord, Slavěna took Dana by the hand and led her, shocked and limping, back to her house and her bees.

* * *

That night Dana got the best night's sleep she'd had in years: no one to worry her with threats or demands or unprovoked, drink-fuelled outbursts. Slavěna had made her a bed with some boards between two benches, and an old straw-stuffed mattress and spare bedclothes, while her dress hung on a hook, dark patches where grime had been damped out, drying in the cosy, stuffy warmth of the cottage.

In the morning they shared some slices of dark rye bread, spread thick with salted butter and the sweetest honey Dana had ever tasted. After this, Slavěna insisted on inspecting Dana's wounds, cleaning them gently with a cloth and warm water from the kettle by the fire. Each cleansing dab stung with pain from the wound itself, but also from the memory of the day before and all the wounds and insults from the weeks and months before that.

Dana was ashamed, but Slavěna ignored that and, in the first gentle tones the woman had heard for years, asked her about her husband and her life and tried not to look appalled by what she said, and how Dana cried.

Slavěna turned the woman's head to one side and inspected the cut under her eye, which had now swollen so much that the eye itself was bruised and hidden, as if behind two pouting lips, smeared with kohl and rouge. Again the injury was cleaned and Slavěna spread a fingertip of honey on the cut.

"Why are you doing that?" asked Dana, content to submit to the ministrations and gentle attention.

"It'll help the cut heal, without scaring", answered her nurse. "It's the magic of the honey". Taking her by the chin, she compared both sides of the woman's face: One was battered and bruised but the other, looking like it belonged to another person entirely, was fine-featured and beautiful. Dana's eye that could still be seen was a deep brown, ringed with black and shot with green flecks, her cheekbones high and delicately pointed, sweeping down the plane of her cheek to a prettily sharp and cleft chin.

Dana's eye looked back into Slavĕna's. "Your eyes – they're so very green".

"They're not always. Sometimes they change – with the seasons", she explained. "They never used to. It's the magic of the honey", she said again. Feeling uncharacteristically shy she looked away. Normally, Slavĕna didn't worry about beautifying herself, but she suddenly felt very self-conscious and retied her hair, tucking stray strands behind her ears.

For Dana, the rest of that day was as if she had found paradise. She relaxed, slept some more, and enjoyed a good lunch and supper with her newfound friend and saviour. She tried to ignore the squirts of anxiety in her belly when she remembered that she would have to face the situation of her husband at some point, until Slavĕna brought up the subject as they sipped medovina by the fire that hissed and popped where unseasoned wood was trying to burn. The drink was dark, sweet and strong and Dana's body and soul felt at ease in this darkened, honeyed sanctuary, and a little of her confidence returned.

"I never want to go back to him", she said after a long pause, staring into the flames and glowing logs. "He has hurt me over and over again and there is nothing I can do too make him stop".

"You shouldn't have to".

"Go back to him or try to make him stop?"

"Both".

Dana picked up the mead jug and, as she topped up their cups, she said, "We were to have a baby once, but he hurt me so badly that I lost it and I've never been able to carry one since".

Both stared at the fire, contemplating this for some time, until Slavěna spoke, "You can stay here if you like – until you're ready to do whatever or go wherever it is you want".

"Thank you".

Not long after this both women got themselves ready for their beds, turning their backs to change and give themselves, and each other, the feeling of privacy.

As Dana hunkered down into her bench-bed Slavěna approached her, holding a pot, but then hesitated.

"What is it?" asked Dana.

Slavěna felt foolish. "My mother", she started, unsure. "When I was small and not well, my mother used to put a little honey on my lips and tell me it would help me sleep and get better. I don't think it ever really did, but it was a nice thing she would do for me. We haven't spoken in a long time. I'm a disappointment".

She turned to go, but Dana reached towards her and said, "I would like that. It might work – it might help my bumps and bruises heal faster, or bring me deep sleep with no dreams: The magic of the honey?" she finished with a smile, recalling her friend's earlier phrase.

Smiling at the shared joke, Slavěna knelt down by the side of Dana's makeshift bed and dipped a finger into the pot and touched a little of the thick, sugary honey onto her guest's lips.

Then both women felt embarrassed at the action and Slavěna moved off quickly to her own bed, while Dana turned over, saying a *good night*, before sucking the mild sweet gold into her mouth.

* * *

The next morning both women felt like they had lived like this forever.

Dana's eye was a little better and had opened somewhat and the two laughed as they prepared breakfast together. Later Slavěna showed Dana how she made the medovina and they both stirred the dark liquid, sweating in the heat and vapour. Some quality control, tasting the strong liquor so early in the day made them both a little giddy and as the sun reached its height, they dozed under the great horse chestnut tree, while its candles blossomed above, and wild forest flowers nodded around them, filling the air with their heady scent, and songbirds with golden throats declaimed their territories and their intentions.

But their idyllic dozing was brought to an abrupt end by the sound of a loud, male voice. It was Dana's husband shouting, demanding to know where she was and hammering on the cottage door. Both women woke from their doze in a panic, hearts thumping, blood racing, and they looked desperately at each other.

"You don't have to go with him if you don't want to", said Slavěna, taking Dana's trembling hand, seeing the woman revert to the shivering kitten she'd first seen.

"I don't want to. I don't want to go with him ever again", was all she could manage.

"Right", said Slavěna determinedly, and got to her feet, striding back towards her cottage. As she arrived, Dana's husband emerged from the inside, followed by another man, who she recognised as one of those who'd been sitting on the drunkard when last they'd met. Unconsciously, she touched the bruise he'd left on the side of her own head and picked up an ash-handled garden hoe as she walked.

"You're not welcome here – go away!" she ordered, continuing her march forward.

Dana's husband wheeled round to face her – the two women clearly weren't the only ones who'd been drinking so early in the day. In fact he still had a bottle of vodka in his hand, from which he swigged, and sneered at her, his lip curling and his eyes – almost the same colour as his drink-fired face – narrowing in hatred. The man behind him smiled apologetically and shrugged his shoulders as if he could do nothing.

"I've come for my wife. Where is she?" the drunkard growled.

"She's not coming with you. You've ruined it. You've ruined her. Now get out of my garden!"

"You don't tell me what to do, you dried up, man-hating spinster", and he started towards her, bunching his fists, but stopped, as Dana stepped up, behind Slavĕna.

In the bravest voice she could manage, the frightened woman spoke. "She's right. I'm not coming back with you. I'm not suffering you anymore. You've beaten me, you killed our child and you're killing me!"

"Oh, I see how it is", said the man, looking between the two women, shrugging off his friend's hand as he tried to pull him away, offering unconvincing conciliatory words. "Two birds in the same bush, eh? I always knew you weren't a proper wife. And you", he turned on Slavĕna, "You're just not a proper woman".

He wasn't ready for the sturdy ash handle of the garden hoe as Slavěna swung it at him. It caught him across the face, connecting with a loud crack and splitting open a gash on his forehead.

"Get out! Get out!" Slavěna roared at him, driving him backwards, still staggering from the blow. But he was ready for the second swing and caught the handle before it could do any real damage. Slavěna wasn't a skilled fighter – in fact she'd never had to fight like this before in her life – but she was driven by fury and fear, and brought her booted foot up between the man's legs and kicked hard, feeling her foot meet his pelvis, and crushing anything in between, judging by the way the man dropped to the ground like a sack of grain.

With an unquestionable command for the other man to take the brawling oaf away before she finished them both, Slavěna scooped her arm protectively round Dana's shoulders and marched them both inside the cottage, and slammed and barred the door.

Slavěna leaned her back against the wood, holding Dana close as the woman sobbed and shook, stroking her hair and allowing her own breathing to begin to slow, listening to the muffled sound of the retreating men outside, the big man's moans interspersed with whining and blurted curses.

The next day was spent as if on a knife's edge, tending to the bees, removing honey from combs, mixing medovina, but also waiting for Dana's husband to come again.

But he didn't.

Nor did he the day after.

Nor the day after that.

Each evening, after they'd made themselves ready for bed it became their little ritual that Slavěna would dab honey onto Dana's mouth and say the words '*It's the magic of the honey*', like a healing prayer.

But the day after *that* the man who'd accompanied Dana's husband knocked on the door of the beekeeper's cottage.

Slavĕna swung the door open, a kitchen knife in her hand, Dana watching cautiously over her shoulder, her wounded eye now fully opened, but surrounded with sickly yellows and stormy blues, her brow creased with worry. Before either woman had a chance to speak the man held up his hands, "I've not come to cause trouble. I've just come to bring some news".

Slavĕna lowered the knife and the women stepped out into early summer sun.

It transpired that, after their last meeting, Dana's husband had gone back to the inn to drown his sorrows in even more drink. After he was told he wouldn't be served any more as he was too drunk for his own good, and driving away other customers, he got angry and pulled out his knife and began threatening the landlord. A scuffle broke out as a number of patrons who'd got fed up with the man's behaviour joined in to help the landlord expel the drunk. In the ensuing fight, Dana's husband fell on his own blade and had died within the hour from the wound.

This man was here to deliver that news and, shrugging as if there was nothing he could do, muttered unconvincing condolences, made his excuses, and left.

Dana wept and wanted to be alone while she grieved for the man who should have been her husband, the marriage they should have had, and the life that should have been theirs.

* * *

After supper they built up the fire and poured and drank a number of cups of medovina.

That night, after both had dressed and were preparing for bed, Slavěna dipped her fingertip into the pot of honey and ran it over Dana's mouth, but as she was about to repeat their phrase, it was Dana who, dipping her own finger into the pot, spread some on Slavěna's lips and said the words, "It's the magic of the honey".

Slavěna looked into Dana' eyes, thinking how rich they were in their brown colouring, like a conker skin, in autumn, and Dana wondered if her companion's eyes seemed less green than before, and now more amber in colour, giving them a golden cast, and both women felt safe and loved.

Maybe it was the medovina, maybe it was the heat from the fire making the cottage drowsy and dreamy, maybe it was the euphoria brought on by Dana's long-awaited freedom, or maybe it was just what was always meant to be, but they brought their honeyed lips together and kissed and felt that nothing and no one else existed in the world.

That night, the first of many nights to come, the women shared one bed, finding a peace, love, tenderness and togetherness neither had found before.

Weeks passed and the two lived as one, happy and content, tending to the garden and the bees, harvesting the honey and making medovina. Spring began to be forgotten as summer brought warmer days and Slavěna noticed how Dana's deep brown eyes now began to show golden flecks – the magic of the honey, they said, and laughed together.

Then Dana found that she did not bleed when she was supposed to. She had already missed one of her cycles and had put it down to the trouble and worry of her husband's brutality and eventual death, but this time she told Slavěna. They talked and Dana said how she couldn't be carrying a child, as her husband's drinking had – for many reasons – meant this had not been possible. But as the weeks went by her belly swelled and her body took on the shapes of motherhood.

Sympathising with the tragedy of her drunken and violent husband, the other villagers supposed the coming baby to be from Dana's late marriage and the two women did nothing to disabuse them of these thoughts, but secretly, they knew the child to be theirs, made possible by the magic of the honey.

Later in the year, when the autumn winds began to blow the leaves from the trees, and Slavěna and Dana found their eyes had become the same earthy brown colour – the brown of bark, and of nuts, and the heads of mushrooms – a child was born to them, in the safety and sanctuary of the beekeepers' cottage: a girl.

They named her Zimolezka – Little Honeysuckle – and thanked the bees and the great horse chestnut tree and, of course, the magic of the honey, for bringing her to them.

She was a happy child with chestnut brown hair, with eyes that, at least for the first few years of her life, until she grew up and left home, changed to match the seasons, like both of her mothers'. She loved the bees and their honey, and the great horse chestnut tree that blossomed in the spring, covered with perfumed, pastel-coloured candles that made such delicious and magical honey and for many years to come the three lived happily together, keeping their bees at the edge of the forest, at the foot of the great tree.

The Hooked Horror and the Forest Girl, Norway

Meanwhile, in Norway, with a mighty sideswipe of his sword, our hero cut another swathe through his adversaries, felling several at once; hack, slash, thrust, parry and slash again. He was a Viking, fierce and proud: an unstoppable berserker, biting the top of his shield to work himself into an invulnerable battle frenzy. Ah-ha! Outflanking him, eh? Nothing that a spinning jump and a scythe-like sweep with his trusty sword *Blood Drinker* wouldn't put a stop to … and then, there he was, standing atop a mound of slain enemies, victorious, panting after his exertions, surveying the gory battlefield.

Imagine the scene.

* * *

Now, when I say 'battlefield', we really mean 'woodland' and when I say 'atop a mound of slain enemies', we really mean 'a patch of nettles', now trampled, battered and flattened by 'his trusty sword *Blood Drinker*', by which I mean a stick of green hazel.

The Viking warriors were all long gone to Valhalla but, when you're seventeen and the best months of the year consist of making *trekull* – charcoal – on your own, in the middle of a forest, there's little else to do but dream.

And Zack was a dreamer.

He dreamt of being a hero, of rescuing princesses – of doing quite a few things with princesses, or girls in general, for that matter – of harnessing the forces of magic, of discovering the hidden treasure hoards of kings, of saving villages from the menaces of ravaging trolls, sweeping down from the mountains or creeping from their caves … of being recognised for the valiant and iron-willed warrior he knew he *could* have been if only he'd been born a few centuries earlier.

And so, often left by himself for hours, or even days, to watch the *trekull branner* – the charcoal fires – in the woodland, he dreamt his dreams and became the hero of his own imagination.

He'd even spent time fortifying the spot in the woodland where his family's charcoal burning happened every summer: he'd dug pits, made palisades of sharpened stakes and built traps, being careful to avoid the paths he and his family used so as not to actually injure anyone who wasn't a bandit or a troll. Zack had also invented various weapons, made from materials to hand, and created costumes and disguises that, one day, might just come in handy.

However, for most of the time, it was an uneventful life for a young man who sought adventure, even though the other lads his age would tease him and tell him what an odd fellow he was with his imagination and his dreams; but here, in the silence of the forest, among his fortifications and with his cash of home-made weapons and artful disguises he could be whatever he liked.

Now, this story is about love, and a young man called Zack; so, now, *re*-imagine the scene…

Imagine yourself in the depths of a forest.

Not a scary, creepy, forest with deep *dark* depths, but just deep within nature, deep in the wilderness and deep among the trees, among the silence, away from the sounds of people, away from the sounds of industry, deep among the trees, where you can be who or whatever you want, or *with* whoever you want, and no one will ever know or bother you, and the days and nights can last forever.

If you were to look around, you would find yourself surrounded by tall, slim trees – pines dripping perfumed resin on their trunks, silver birch with their peeling paper bark, the sturdy straight trunks and limbs of the ash, their broad leaves fluttering in a light summer breeze, and the feathered little leaves and bright orange berries of the rowan – all good for harvesting and allowing to smoulder in a woodland alchemy, until they become charcoal.

Deep in the woods, among the trees, Zack's predecessors had made a clearing.

To make *trekull* you first make a stack of cut and dried wood and set it on fire. But, just setting the stack alight would simply reduce the valuable wood to valueless ash, so to make sure this doesn't happen you'd cover the wood with earth, to smother it, allowing only a small amount of oxygen in. For some days the wood smoulders under the great mound with thin ribbons of smoke spiralling up from the heated earth, filling the forest with that distinctive and delicious smell of wood smoke.

Now, to make sure the fire neither dies nor takes over, there must be someone on hand, day and night, to watch, and this was Zack's job. It was an important job, but not a very exciting one.

On this particular day, with little else to do, as the sun started to head towards the horizon, Zack made his rounds of the camp – the place where his family had made charcoal since his great grandfather's day – before pottering about, inspecting his traps and swinging his 'sword' around, until he grew tired.

The most difficult part was at night. The temptation to sleep was strong and so, under a shelter that kept him dry if it rained, he would sit on a one-legged stool, a traditional item, used by charcoal burners. A round wooden seat would be supported by a single, central leg, meaning Zack could rest, but any time he got close to nodding off, he would loose concentration and balance and so, starting to tip over, would wake himself up.

To stop himself from getting bored, he busied himself in front of the little fire he'd lit, tending to the wood-cutting tools: the felling axes, the hatchets and the *laukniver* – the bill hooks: multipurpose, flat, broad, hooked blades for chopping or stripping off small branches.

But, eventually – as we all expected he would – Zack began to nod and, as he did he began to tip to one side or the other, on his one-legged stool and woke himself up, with a start. After several of these near collapses, Zack decided that a walk around the camp would be better than sleep-deprived stool-wobbling.

Building up the little campfire, he lit his lantern and inspected the smoking mounds. All seemed well with the miniature hills, the heat and thin spirals of smoke made him feel like a giant, striding between volcanoes and he altered his step accordingly to complete the illusion.

Striding around and peering theatrically at the air vents, Zack suddenly froze at a sound from the forest. He didn't move, holding his breath, listening intently in the dark silence of the forest night. No … nothing.

He relaxed and was just about the straighten up, when there it was again – this time it was real, for sure: A woman's scream and shouts of distress, away in the darkness. He had to do something – he had spent years preparing for things that *just might happen* and now they definitely *were* happening!

He grabbed the things he needed and, closing the shutters on his lantern so that it showed the very minimum amount of light needed to pick his way through the midnight forest, he plunged into the darkness, fear and excitement pumping his legs as he sprinted off towards the woman's intermittent shouts, which guided his hero's flight.

* * *

What happened next is probably best told from the perspective of two thieves.

Having ambushed a young woman who was foolishly travelling the forest alone, at dusk, the two thieves had gone deeper into the woods and set up camp. Clearly, the young woman's fear had waned a few hours after her capture, as the thieves had done nothing to her person, but bind her hands and tie them behind the trunk of a young tree. Eventually she had plucked up courage enough to scream out and shout for help. One of them had slapped her hard across the face and told her to shut up, and that had kept her quiet for a while.

They had been through her basket and, while they'd found some good food and strong drink, there was little else there and certainly nothing of value. They'd rifled through her cloak and even undone her stays and, much to her fear and anger, rummaged inside her bodice as well, but had yet to find anything, so while one built up their campfire, adding more dry wood and making the flames leap, the other continued to go through her clothing.

Grinning and sniggering at the young woman, the thief prepared to go through her dress and her petticoats, but before he had a chance, and the young woman was thankful for the interruption for more reasons than may be immediately apparent right now, the sound of a snapping twig at the edge of the firelight made all three whip their heads round to see who was there.

While the fire crackled and spat tall, yellow, licking flames, that sent sparks rising in spirals up and into the darkness of the forest canopy, at the edge of the halo of ghostly light stood a figure. It was cloaked from head to toe in black, with a black hood and long black sleeves that covered the figure's hands. As the thieves and the young woman watched the dark spectre raised its cowled head to show two smouldering red eyes, glowing from the depths of the hood. The thieves now watched in terror as the wraith lifted its arms across and up in front of its body, and with the sound of swords being drawn from their sheaths, it held its arms aloft, the folds of black cloth falling back to reveal that, where hands should have been, the creature instead had curved, flat-bladed metal hooks!

Then the apparition spoke, declaiming loudly, "Se! Jeg er den hekta skrekk!" – *Behold! I am the hooked horror!*

The two thieves started to scramble away, to the furthest edge of the circle of firelight, but the awful thing came on, its eyes glowing ferociously, its hooked hands glinting wickedly in the flames, and it spoke again, heading for the young woman tied to the tree, and helpless, "I am pleased that you have brought me this sacrifice!"

As it continued to speak it slipped one of its deadly looking hooks into the rope, binding its victim to the tree, and sliced through her bonds and then pulled her towards itself, retreating into the shadows of the midnight forest, backing away with the woman in its bladed grasp.

"I will now take this offering back to my lair of doom and slice her and devour her at my leisure over a hundred darkened nights!"

Open-mouthed, the thieves watched the murderous fiend start to recede into the shadows of the trees, quaking and thankful that it wasn't them that the Hooked Horror had taken.

It was all going perfectly.

And then it stopped going perfectly.

As he'd reached the young woman and sliced, rather dramatically he felt, through the ropes that held her, Zack – for, of course, the Hooked Horror was Zack, in one of his disguises that he had had ready for something that *just might happen* – he'd whispered words of comfort to the young woman, "I'm here to rescue you – just play along".

But, the smouldering twigs that he'd threaded through the fabric to create the effect of glowing eyes had filled his hood with wood smoke and now his real eyes were streaming and he could see almost nothing but the blur of the firelight, twinkling through the smoky tears. Next, as he made his retreat, away from the thieves' camp, the bottom of his voluminous robes caught on a bramble on the forest floor. As he backed away into the darkness, his arms wrapped possessively around his supposed sacrificial victim, his gown was pulled off him, like a magician, pulling a tablecloth away and leaving a dinner set standing. This time, however, it just revealed a rather gangly youth, holding a *laukniv* – a billhook – in each hand.

There was a pause and then several things happened at once: Zack froze, his young face a mask of white fear; the thieves, realising they'd been duped, roared in anger, and rose to the their feet in pursuit, scrabbling for their weapons; and, the most sensible among them, the young woman, shouted, "*Run!*"

Zack and the young woman crashed through the darkened trees and scratching, tearing undergrowth, the thieves hot on their trail, bellowing threats and curses. It was dark and rough going for all, but Zack knew this part of the forest well – he travelled and explored it every day – and suddenly pulled the young woman in a particular direction, calling out over his shoulder for her to trust him.

Stronger, with greater stamina and driven by their anger, the thieves were gaining and the two young people knew this, when suddenly Zack called over his shoulder, "Get ready to jump!"

Still wondering what he meant, the young woman heard Zack almost whisper the words "Jump – *now*!" and, like him, she leapt over what seemed nothing more than a wide circle of leaves on the forest path, but soon heard behind her a cracking of sticks and the sound of the nearest thief falling into a concealed pit and crying out in pain.

Trap-running, zigzag along the night-forest paths, Zach hoped he was still going where he thought he was, when he felt his ankle pull against something crossing the path – a tripwire he'd set – and shouted "Duck!" The young woman, learning from her rescuer's previous instruction crouched as she ran, only too feel something whoosh over her in the dark and connect with their final pursuer, with a muffled cry and a thumping crack that made her wince.

Slowing to catch their breath, Zack told his companion that he'd take her to safety by a roundabout route, in case either of her assailants still felt like following, and they walked in silence through the night, finally picking their way between Zack's fortifications as they entered the charcoal burning camp and, exhausted, they sat on the floor, on some cloth that Zack produced, and refreshed themselves with the remnants of Zack's supplies.

During this time, the young woman thanked Zack and told him her name was Britt. He blushed, as she told him how clever and brave he'd been in rescuing her, and muttered dismissive thanks into his boots. With no sign of the thieves they began to relax and talked about this and that. Although he was smart, Zack was not very worldly-wise and a little naïve, and when the conversation strayed towards who Britt was, where she came from and why she had been walking alone in the forest at night, she gently sidestepped the questions, before steering the subject back to Zack and *his* life, and so the conversation continued late into the small hours.

* * *

It was with a start that Zack woke up.

It was almost fully daylight so he must have been asleep for some hours. Groggily, he cried out an unintelligible sound of alarm and began to struggle to sit up, but Britt was still there with him. She had been cradling his sleeping head in her lap and, with soothing tones she reassured him that everything was alright and that she had tended the *trekull branner* – the charcoal fires – as her people had experience with such things, but it was time for her to go, as Zack's father would be along soon.

She thanked him again, pecking him on the cheek, which stirred all sorts of feelings within Zack and he became quiet discombobulated. As she walked away, waving goodbye, he blurted, "Can I see you again?"

She paused, thinking for a moment, then turned and looked earnestly at him with a great seriousness in her eyes that Zack didn't understand. "Are you sure?" she asked with a little frown.

"Yes!" he replied, perhaps, a little too enthusiastically.

She smiled at his keenness. "When are you next watching the fires?"

"Three days' time – I arrive just after dawn".

"Then I'll see you in three days' time, just after dawn. I'll bring some soup; and *this* time I'll be more careful where I walk". Turning and giving a wave over her shoulder, Britt disappeared among the trees, into the sunny dapples of the forest.

For the next three days Zack could think of nothing else but his forthcoming assignation. He couldn't sleep, he barely ate, he couldn't concentrate on anything, and he certainly couldn't bring himself to mention to his family what had happened in the depths of the midnight forest – his rescue, the independent forest girl and their plans to meet again. In fact, he rather suspected his parents wouldn't approve of a girl who went around alone at night and made arrangements to meet boys, without a chaperone, but he didn't care: This was an adventure and, by wit and bravery he had won his chance to rescue his very own – almost – princess.

But despite the feeling that the day would never come, of course it eventually did, and in a drizzling grey near-dawn he said goodbye to his tired father who'd just finished the overnight shift, did a quick check of the smoking earthen mounds and then ducked under the small shelter and waited for Britt to arrive.

The minutes dragged in the humid clearing, as heavy drops fell from the shelter's roof, plopping onto the bare ground – a mixture of soil, leaf litter and sooty charcoal ash. The warm smells of the forest rose with the sun – wet bark, green bracken, thick mushrooms – and the treetops started to steam.

In the midst of that intoxicatingly green atmosphere, Zack felt his heart surge as Britt stepped out of the mists, her long, sage-green skirts brushing the tips of the grass, her bodice criss-cross laced across a linen blouse, and a white kerchief, with colourful embroidery on its borders, tied about her head. She smiled shyly and waved to Zack with her free hand, the other carrying a basket, covered with a cloth.

As the summer sun rose, burning off the verdant mists and sending green-mottled showers of twinkling light into the clearing, the two chatted and laughed about the other night, about how horrible the experience had been, and how clever, brave – and funny – Zack had been.

Later, the young man took Britt on a tour of the charcoal burning camp and he was surprised by how much she already knew about the craft – something her people had a good knowledge of, she said.

As Zack's time in the forest came to the end, that day, they said their goodbyes and, holding hands, they kissed, rather awkwardly and shyly, but nevertheless their kiss felt to Zack like the first kiss the world had known and no other kiss would ever be as passionate or mean as much as *their* first kiss together, and his first kiss … ever.

His body humming with pride and pleasure, and suffused with teenaged appetites, Zack and Britt arranged to meet the next time he was at the camp – at sun-up, two mornings hence.

* * *

Again they met, again they sat and talked and again they kissed. As the sun crept towards the treetops and Zack's shift was coming to an end, he waved goodbye to Britt, his feelings for her growing to an almost insufferable strength, surging in his body. Just as she was reaching the edge of the camp, about to vanish back into the forest, among the trees, Zack saw something that made him gasp. At this sound, Britt span round, but too late, she realised what Zack had seen: Poking out from under the back of her skirts was a tail, like a cow's, covered in red-brown fur and finished with a brush of black hair.

Britt stood, frozen to the spot, tucking her tail behind her, her cheeks flushing bright red.

Zack knew what she was – she wasn't a human girl, she was a *hulder*, one of the 'hidden ones': Legends spoke of how these women who were descended from an ancient race, started when a woman had washed only half of her children when God came to her cottage and, ashamed of the dirty ones, she hid them. God decreed that those she had hidden from him would be hidden from humanity, and they became the hulders, friends of woodsmen, and could bring luck or misfortune depending on how they were treated.

Aware of the threat of bad luck, but also filled with a genuine love for the young hulder, as the two young people stood still, their gaze locked together, Zack, to his surprise, offered up an explanation: "Britt, my love, it is just that your petticoat was showing at the back of your skirts, that is all – nothing to be alarmed at".

Britt relaxed a little and smiled. "After you've seen my 'petticoats', young sir, are you still of a mind for me to visit you in two days' time?" she asked, raising an eyebrow and waiting, desperately hoping for the answer she wanted to hear.

"Yes, of course", grinned Zack. "And every other day and night you can come to me".

"Then I shall see you in two days' time". She smiled, turned and with a little skip of pleasure, her tail bouncing behind her, walked back into the woods.

* * *

Over the next couple of days Zack had plenty to think about. He had to think about Britt the *girl* and also Britt the *hulder*, but whenever he thought about anything difficult or his mind started to cloud with doubt, he thought about their kisses; and when he thought about their kisses, any of those confusing or doubtful thoughts disappeared like wood smoke on a summer's breeze, and he found himself unable to wait for his next meeting with Britt.

Again, despite his feverish, lovesick sleepless nights and scant meals, the twilight time for going to the woods eventually came. Zack's parents asked him why he was dressed in such good clothes for watching the charcoal fires – didn't he know that that day his father had raked open some of the *jordovner* – the earth kilns – and that his good clothes would get covered in soot? But Zack said that it was always best to keep up good appearances so that people thought well of the family, and his parents couldn't argue with this, so off he went, this time with a flask of the best ale and a freshly baked cake. His parents – quite rightly, and with much supressed pride and excitement – suspected he was going to meet a girl. Zack, of course thought his parents suspected nothing and was puzzled when his mother called out "Be *careful*!" and his father followed up with a simple "You know", and that was all that was said.

* * *

The young couple kissed as they met and then spent the first part of the evening trying on the various costumes and disguises that Zack had made and hidden in preparation for defence or attack. There was the cloak for the hooked horror, which Britt now tried on, and ran around making ghostly *wooooooo!* noises, along with a shambling mess of tattered rags and dried bracken, attached to an old fishing net, that would have made the wearer invisible if they'd remained stationary in the undergrowth – Zack called this his 'forest lurker' outfit, although now that he said it out loud it sounded more than a little creepy. There were even some stilts with extra long trousers and a large and grotesque papier-mâché head, but Zack said he wasn't very good on the stilts and found great difficulty getting upright on them, let alone walking about and making himself into a convincing troll, but it gave them both something to laugh at together as they played with the huge mask.

All through this and the inspection of the various spears, catapults, pit traps, deadfalls and trip wires, the two young people laughed and joked and teased each other, running through the forest, now painted in monochrome light and shadow by a full, lovers' moon.

Tired from their play, and thirsty, they sat on the ground, in the moonlight, leaning their backs against the warm earthen mounds, and shared Zack's flask of ale, feeling its strong, perfumed warmth spreading delightfully through their limbs. Looking down, Zack could see Britt's hulder tail. For a moment she looked nervously at him, until he haltingly asked, "May I touch it?"

She nodded and, gingerly, Zack stroked his fingertips down the short red-brown fur of its length, feeling the individual bones inside, reminding him of stroking his cat's tail or running one's finger down someone's back, and then he let the hair on the tail's end pass through his palm.

They looked again at each other and kissed; this time with a deeper passion – this time with a hunger for each other and, lying against the warm, smoking mounds of the earth kilns they entwined.

* * *

Later, as they lay in each other's arms, careless of the soot and smoke that covered them, their clothes in disarray, they were peaceful and content, talking softly of the moon and its face, as it smiled down upon them, while Zack wove ferns into Britt's long, golden hair and she smiled into his eyes.

Slowly their talk turned to what was to become of them, that a hulder and a human man couldn't be together – that their respective people and families would never allow it and then made promises that they would never separate and never be apart and that they loved each other and their differences didn't matter and that love would conquer all.

But as they made these vows to each other and to the moon and turned to embrace, their arms around the other, Zack suddenly pulled away in surprise and horror.

"What!" said Britt in shock and worry, searching Zack's face for an answer.

"Your back", was all that Zack could say. Britt's face fell into a mask of despair as she nodded and, turning away from him, lifted her linen blouse to reveal her back.

Where smooth young skin should have stretched from shoulders to hips, instead her back lay open and hollow, like the trunk of a tree, rent by lightning, and through the bark-edged split that ran half the length of her young back, Zack could see that it was like looking into a hollow log.

Zack tried to swallow his repulsion and muttered platitudes, but Britt could hear the truth in his stammering voice. Clearly, a girl with a tail was one thing, but a girl who was a forest child and of the trees was another.

Britt began to sob.

She pulled her blouse around her, laced up her bodice and stood, her face besmirched by soot where tears had run mournful tracks down her cheeks. With a look of such pain and such misery she turned and ran into the forest, tearing the ferns from her hair as she went.

Gathering himself, and shaking his head to clear it, Zack scrambled to his feet and sprinted after Britt. He followed the main track, but couldn't see any sign of her; he doubled back and looked for places where she might have left the path, calling out her name, into the moon-shadowed woods, but there was no reply and he could find no trace of where she'd passed.

After many minutes of running and searching and crying out Britt's name, Zack gave up. He leaned against the tall, straight trunk of a pine, catching his breath and then began to cry, great, racking sobs – he knew that his first love had come and gone, and he would never see Britt again.

* * *

As with a lot of things that happen in a teenager's life, Zack's parents never knew what had happened – what their son had found and lost in the midnight forest.

Even though there was never a reply, nor sign that she had passed that way, whenever Zack was on duty at the *trekullbranner leir* – the charcoal burners' camp – he scouted the edge of the clearing, peered deep into the green shadows and, sometimes, when he thought he'd seen a movement, the silhouette of a girl, or the turn of a sage-green skirt between the unmoved and unloving trunks of the trees, he'd call out for Britt. And each time he called, it was with a voice a little quieter and little less hopeful than before. Eventually he stopped calling altogether and, as the days became weeks and the weeks became months, Britt, the hulder, became like a dream and he began to wonder if she'd ever been real.

* * *

Quietly, summer came to a close and, tired of life, began to change from green to brown, turning over in it's coverlet of falling leaves and the forest began its winter sleep.

With the season for making charcoal gone for the old year and yet to start in the new, Zack's work and duties kept him closer to home and for this he was thankful as he tried – and failed – to forget Britt.

* * *

But when the land began to stir and mutter in its slumber with the first wakings of spring it was his mother who found the baby boy.

'A foundling', his family always said later, although when the boy grew he *clearly carried his father's looks, sprinkled with a little magic*, as Zack's mother always said with a knowing look. He arrived one morning, sleeping peacefully in a basket of woven wicker, outside the family's front door, wrapped in a cloth of green sage and lying on a bed of green forest ferns.

He was taken in by Zack and his family, and loved for the boy he grew up to be, no matter who or where he had come from. He always had an affinity with the forest, knowing the seasons and the plants and the animals – where to find a nest of eggs, or where the squirrels slept in winter, or the best places to track and hunt boar; his hair was the colour of brown bark and his eyes the colour of green hazel.

Who his mother was, nobody knew, but his 'older brother' Zack, from who he was inseparable, would make up stories of how she was a forest maiden, full of beautify and magic, and that was enough for both of them.

The Angel's Feather, Winchester, Kingdom of Wessex [England]

There are two things you need to know: Firstly that Judd was going to become a monk, and secondly that it had just begun to snow.

On becoming a monk, Judd was clear on this, and there were certain reasons why he was going to be a monk: He loved God, as all good people did, but there was something that he loved almost as much as God – even more, if he were truly honest, and his tutor, a priest, wasn't listening – and it was this thing he loved that made him want to become a monk.

Judd was sixteen – a young man – and the girl, about his age, who was standing opposite him, as the heavy flakes began to drift down around them and the ground sparkled, was going to help him achieve his dream. Lying in her open hands, was the artefact she had brought him, as promised, and it was this that was going to help him indulge his true love.

Now, Judd *liked* to read; he *liked* to unroll the parchments and see the histories, the documents, charters and letters – the stories – unfold. He liked to take the big, heavy books down from the shelves in the monastery library, their chains clattering, feeling the slight give and softness in the thick, leather covers and open them on the lecterns, pouring over the vellum pages filled with delicately calligraphed lettering, illustrated with beautifully rich, colourful pictures of Bible scenes, kings, warriors and fabulous animals from distant lands, and to gaze at the illuminated letters, sumptuous and glowing with gold leaf.

But even more than liking to read, Judd loved to write.

He loved to write because he could – and not many he knew could say that – but Judd loved to write most of all because he enjoyed the confluence of artistry and history. When a person wrote they created beautiful pictures with lines, strokes and flicks, and simultaneously they captured real moments in time – real moments involving real people, in real places: great deeds and turning points in the history of mankind; they captured stories of kings and heroes, of saints and martyrs, of God and Angels.

Judd was going to become a monk, because he loved God, but, more importantly, so he could write.

His father, Hlaford, a well-to-do low-ranking nobleman, owner of land and serfs, and commander of warriors had had Judd taught to read and write when he was twelve – something *he* had never learned. Seeing as the King seemed to think it was important to read and write, everyone else who also wanted to be seen as important now also thought it was important and, while it was too late for many of the adults, the sons and daughters of moneyed families were educated by monks and priests in this skill.

Judd's father didn't *really* approve and thought that while it was fine for girls to be educated, boys ought to be working or fighting or finding out what educated girls were all about; but he loved his son.

Despite his exasperation with Judd's habit of spending time … *reading and writing* … if the King approved, then doing things the King approved of was a good start towards a peaceful and prosperous life and that was what he wished for his son.

What he didn't wish for though, was for his son to be a monk – he'd hoped his son would take over the family estate, give him fine strong grandchildren and help enforce the peace with the Danes. Judd, however, was quite clear that he wanted to become a monk, to spend his days in service to God, reading and writing.

This age-old tension between father and son who wanted different things often led Judd, an only child, to wander the countryside by himself, deep in his own thoughts.

It had been a few years since the peace treaty with the Danes – the Vikings – who now held most of England north of Wessex under what was called Danelaw, so the countryside was relatively safe and patrols of Saxon warriors kept any bands of raiders or bandits at bay. Besides, Judd, as the son of a nobleman had been given his first sword at the age of thirteen and now, at sixteen, was both reasonably proficient in its use and fleet of foot enough to escape from most danger.

Less of a worry than attack by marauding Danes, but more mysterious to Judd, were the ruins.

Local lore had it that the building Judd liked to visit was once a temple to a pagan god, worshipped by the semi-legendary Romans – a people from a far-off land who had invaded England with their seemingly unstoppable armies, their heavy armour and almost unimaginable machines that could launch spears like a bow launched arrows, or flung stones the size of a man's head. Why they had left no one seemed sure, but the evidence of their presence was to be found, dotting the English countryside, stone piled upon stone to make their once mighty buildings, whereas the good Saxon folk made their houses and their halls from wood and thatch.

On one of his walks Judd found himself at the ruins again. He liked to go there to think deep thoughts about life: about what he would become, what he wanted to be and what the world meant, as many teenagers do. It was a bright, dry winter day and the pale stone blocks stood out from the withered brown grass, glossy green ivy and scrubby trees that were trying to reclaim and pull them the back into the bosom of the earth. Stepping over a pile of smaller pieces, he headed to his favourite spot, where one particularly large block of marble made a convenient seat for him to look at what had once been a carved frieze. The pictures that stood out from this stone he often felt drawn to were of a woman in flowing robes, who held a lyre in one hand and an open scroll in the other. He often felt as if this carved woman called to him in some way and he would spend a long time looking at the shape of her, in the stone, wondering what she would have said if she could speak, and what was written on the weathered scroll she held out; he wondered if the carving was of a real woman or of an imagined demigod, wondered if she had ever stood where he was now, looking at her own image, made immortal in stone.

"Hello", said a voice behind him, making him jump.

It was Elvia. She often found him here. She would see him walking along the skyline of the hills, from her home, and so would come and meet him here and talk.

"You're always looking at that carving", she observed, coming to sit next to Judd and budging up against him to make him make more room for her to sit down.

"She's beautiful", replied Judd simply. "I wonder who she was – if she was ever real."

"Are you in love with her?" teased Elvia.

"No I am not!" Judd replied hotly, his cheeks flushing red.

He got up and went to pointedly examine some other detail of the ruins.

Also sixteen, Elvia's blue eyes sparkled as she smiled to herself, enjoying Judd's discomfort. She took a bite out of the apple she'd got from the food store at home, wiping the sweet juice off her lips, deep pink in contrast to her pale skin, and tucked some errant curls from her cascade of red hair behind an ear, as she watched Judd's contrived distraction.

"Have you told your father?" she asked, breaking the companionable silence, before taking another crunching bite.

"That I'm going to become a monk?"

"No, not that. I know you've told him that and he doesn't like it. I meant about the King's man looking for scribes and you wanting to try out for that?" Another bite.

"He doesn't know yet. I read the notice in the town, but as he can't read, he didn't understand it. I've told my tutor and he thinks I'm good enough, but I'm not sure."

Elvia munched thoughtfully on her apple, watching the young man, an internal struggle taking place in him before he spoke again. "If I could become a scribe for a bit, I might learn how to make the beautiful illuminated letters that the King would surely need on his documents, so that when I went into the monastery I'd be allowed to write manuscripts and even books".

He turned to face her, "I'm going to become a monk".

"You sure?" asked Elvia, pointing at the cracked marble frieze, lying in the grass, a snail climbing slowly up one edge. "What happens if your beautiful woman turns up and you're a monk and you can't marry her?"

"Shut up!" started Judd, defensively. "I'm not in love with her! Anyway – there aren't any women around here who'd be interested in me, I'm not a warrior, I'm a scribe … or at least I will be one day … what woman would be interested in someone like me?"

Elvia gently lobbed her apple core at Judd. Crossly he jumped out of the way.

"What was that for?" he asked.

"Really?" she said, but the young man had no idea what she meant.

Shaking her head and muttering something about *boys*, Elvia hopped off the marble block, brushing her skirts down and started to head off towards her home.

"Tell your Father what you want, and then one day you'll become a monk", she called over her shoulder, throwing him a wave.

Judd stood in the centre of the ruins, looking again at the woman in the carving, with her lyre and the scroll, as the shadows lengthened and winter's chill nibbled the air, before he in turn walked home.

* * *

The conversation with his father saddened him, but what teenaged lad had ever been put off by someone else's lack of vision, when it came to their own destiny.

Hlaford heard what his son had to say and, after expressing his desire that he would really rather that he took on some of the estate and improved the family name, he conceded that if that was what Judd wanted and God had called him to a monastic life of letters, that this test was an opportunity to help him on his way and yes, he would pay for his tutor to give him extra lessons in preparation.

This first hurdle being cleared more easily than Judd had imagined, he now found his next problem was aching self-doubt, and this he confided when he next met Elvia at the ruins. She listened, her head cocked on one side, as Judd talked about his concerns and worries about his ability to pass the writing test that he had now agreed to undertake and that was happening a few days before Yule: He had to receive dictation from one of the King's men to see how quickly and accurately he could record spoken word, as well as bring with him a piece of writing he had prepared in his own time. He spoke of his fears and inadequacies but how he was sure it was God's will that he must become a competent scribe, if he was worthy, before trailing off, shrugging and dropping himself down, despondently next to his friend. She scrubbed her fingers through his hair, as if he were a favourite puppy and then jumped up, facing him.

She lifted up his chin up to look at his pathetic, sad face. "Stop being a pudding", she commanded. "You've got great skill and can do this", but Judd just sighed.

"And", she continued. "I've got something that will help you: A holy relic; a real holy relic that will help you".

At this, the young man brightened up. His tutor had talked of such things – the bones of saints, splinters of the true cross and any number of things that carried the power of God within them.

"Meet me here same time tomorrow and I'll have something for you that'll mean you'll be the best scribe ever and, God willing, one day you'll become a monk".

Judd, grinning, gave her a hug, which Elvia returned warmly, before running off, calling farewells as she went.

* * *

The next day, among the ruins, as the cold, crisp afternoon came towards its close, Judd and Elvia stood facing each other. It was nearly Yuletide and the snow had just begun to fall from leaden clouds, pierced by a shining winter sun, as the young woman stretched her arms forward, her open hands side by side, palms facing up, carrying the holy relic she had promised to bring.

She had given a rather complicated explanation of where the object had come from and confusingly intricate reasoning as to how she knew it to be genuine that had left the young man baffled, but convinced, and there, in her hands, Elvia offered her friend a pure white feather from an Angel's wing.

"It's beautiful", he whispered. "Just like a swan or goose feather ... but there's a radiance about it that's ... that's holy". Elvia nodded and made a positive sounding, but noncommittal noise.

"A feather from the wing of an Angel! May I touch it?" he asked.

"Touch it?" she replied, now sounding exasperated. "Touch it, you pudding? You're to cut a pen from it and let God decide whether you'll become a monk or not. Take it – it's yours. I give this ... to you". And she presented the young man with the feather.

Judd gently took it and held it up, among the whirling snowflakes, so that the early evening light turned it from pure white to burning gold.

"Yes ... thank you ... I will. I'll cut a pen from this Angelic relic and then I pray that God will guide my hand in the test".

Elvia smiled, but avoided Judd's eyes.

* * *

At home, Judd had spent many days looking at the feather, sharping a small knife and almost introducing the two, over and over again, before putting one or both down. He felt he knew what a jeweler must feel like, knowing that one mistake might split a precious stone and render it worthless.

He normally used a stylus made from a stiff reed for his writing, but had been allowed to try his tutor's quill pens and been instructed in how to manufacture one himself.

Yuletide and the test were approaching fast, so, stiffening his resolve, he made a short prayer, before picking up his knife, stripping back the soft feathers, denuding the quill and leaving only a diamond-shaped block of the vane feather at one end, before carving a scoop and cutting a nib with a split at the other.

It was done.

The Angel feather was cut into a pen.

With a trembling hand, he dipped the pen into an inkpot. He settled the nib onto a fresh sheet of velum and with a stroke that started gently and then pressed harder he created the first sweep of an 'A', the first letter that spelled out the words 'Ad Maiorem Dei Gloriam' – 'To the Greater Glory of God'.

He was ready.

* * *

Despite the brittle sunlight outside, the antechamber was dimly lit with candles. Apart from Judd there were three other people in the room: One was another young man, maybe in his early twenties, one still just a boy – probably the same age as Judd has been when he had learned to read and write. The third man was a grim-faced soldier, standing in front of the doors that led into the main chamber.

Judd was used to being around his father's men – they made him feel safe, they knew him and would joke with him – but this man was someone else's warrior and as such had no jokes or larks to play with him, but instead stood on guard with his spear, the butt of its haft resting on the ground and a circular shield, painted with a geometric pattern, on his other arm. The guard wore a chainmail shirt, over a coat of thick, padded armour, made from layers of tough linen, quilted and stuffed with wool. Tall, powerfully built and thickly bearded, the guard glowered from under his helm and pointedly ignored the three nervous individuals who sat silently on benches.

Looking back at the others, Judd worried that he was either too young or too old. Whichever of the others he looked at he decided they'd be much better qualified, more experienced or just more talented. But then he remembered the feather, and squeezed the soft leather bundle that was on his lap, containing this holy artefact as well as his own piece of writing to show, and he felt comforted.

After some time waiting in anxious silence the doors opened, the guard stepping aside. The man who entered was important – anyone could see that. He wore a deep red garment that covered his upper body, down to his knees, with bleached white leggings, deep ochre-coloured bindings around his calves, and leather shoes. The chain of office around his neck confirmed his status as an ealdorman and, with great authority he told the three to follow him into the room beyond.

* * *

First, the ealdorman inspected the writing they had brought with them. He huffed at the young boy's, raised his eyebrows at the other young man's work, but simply looked at Judd's piece of ecclesiastical devotion and said the word "good".

Next came the test. Judd's heart almost stopped when they were given reed styluses to go with ink and fresh velum, but, timidly, he asked if he were allowed to use the quill he'd brought with him and the man simply shrugged in agreement.

Then the ealdorman began to speak and all three began to write.

* * *

After it was finished Judd had no idea how the test had gone. He felt he'd done what was asked, but was also plagued by doubt.

However just as Yule was about to begin, on the eve of Christmas a boy had arrived at his father's hall with a message, a message befitting its purpose and so written on a small scroll and sealed.

Judd had run up the hill, through the snowy white landscape and through the falling flakes to the ruins and impatiently paced back and forth in front of the frieze with the woman with the lyre and scroll, hoping Elvia would have seen him from her father's farm in the valley.

Stamping his feet to keep out the chill, Judd didn't have to wait long before he saw Evlia's red hair against the snowy fields in the distance, as his friend trudged up the hill.

"So?" she asked, leaning on her knees to catch her breath.

Mutely Judd held out the scroll.

"I'm not reading it, you pudding – you're the one who wants to become a monk, you're the one who took the test to become a royal scribe, you're the one who should read it".

With trembling hands, the young man broke the seal and read the contents.

Elvia felt her heart drop as Judd's face turned white, his arm dropped to his side and his chin sunk to his chest. She reached out and pulled him close, feeling her own tears welling in sympathy at his disappointment.

"Never mind", she said, hugging him tightly and scrubbing her hand through his hair. "I'm sure he monastery will still be very pleased to have someone of your talent in the scriptorium".

"It's not that", Judd interrupted, pulling away from her a little. "I passed. They want me to become a scribe for King Ælfrēd. I did it", he finished limply, unable to believe it.

"Pudding!" shouted Elvia thumping him on the shoulder. "I could murder you! I thought you hadn't done it! I knew you could do it! I knew it!"

A slow smile crept across Judd's face as the realisation sunk in.

"I'm going to become a scribe. Then I'm going to become a monk. I'm going to write and I can do it all day every day if I want and I'll even get paid to do it".

The two young people stood smiling, laughing and hugging each other as the silent snow settled all around them.

"I really couldn't have done it without your Angel's feather", smiled Judd, taking Elvia's hands in his, while she smiled and shrugged without answering.

"No", he corrected himself. "I couldn't have done it without you. How can I ever repay you?" he asked, shaking his head in wonder at the young woman.

A few moments passed in silence, each looking at the other, before Elvia quietly answered, "A kiss might be a start?"

Judd felt like he'd been struck by a thunderbolt. Well, yes, he'd thought about Elvia in that way, but he was going to become a monk and anyway she wouldn't be interested in him like that … would she?

With snowflakes landing on their lashes and cheeks the two young people pulled each other close … and they kissed; a kiss that felt like it could have lasted for forever and a day in the snow-blanketed winter silence.

* * *

In the time that followed Judd did *not* become a monk. Instead he *did* become a scribe and advisor to Ælfrēd, King of Wessex, and got to read and write every day.

It also pleased everyone, including his father, that Judd and Elvia married and stayed very much in love for the rest of their days. Their children went on into the world to find their own paths, adventures and loves and Elvia was able to supply Judd with as many fine goose quills from her father's farm, as he desired.

That year and for many to come it was, as the Saxons would have said, a good Yule and, as we say today, a very Merry Christmas.

King's Hill Farm, West coast of Ireland

Seán was born and grew up in his parents' pub in East Point, in Dublin's docklands, but it was always his grandfather's stories of farming the open spaces of the hills and mountains of Wales that made him yearn to have his own farm one day.

After his parents had died, Seán and wife Aoife had taken on the management of the pub, *The Mermaid's Purse*. A good publican and a canny businessman, Seán turned what was already a profitable hostelry into a busy and thriving concern. When their children, a girl and a boy, Fia and Colm, were born, Seán and Aoife began to reflect on the challenges of raising little ones in the hustle and bustle of the quayside pub and weighed them against the rapidly growing savings they were accumulating. With two young children to look after, and working long hours to support the growing business, the couple made the decision to sell up and find a life less hectic, and enjoy some of the profits of their labours.

While clippers and big square-rigger ships rocked at anchor, just outside, swaying to the slow and stately rhythm of the tides, their sails furled and bound, Seán conducted some research over the bar and over a few pints, with the many familiar patrons who passed through, on business.

It didn't take long to identify a farm for sale: about as far south and west as the land would stretch. It was a very good price and before its owner, an old man, had died last year, it had been a very successful mixed farm of oats and sheep, high on the cliffs, with its own stretch of beach, and sheltered from the Atlantic winds, being set on the lee, as the land sloped down and away from the cliff top. Why no one else had bought it, the man couldn't say but it may have been because of its remoteness from the now thriving cities and ports that were drawing more and more people away from the countryside every year.

Always with an eye for a good deal, '*a businessman, not a fighter*', as Seán would often say, letters were quickly written proposing an offer under the asking price, but with the promise of a quick and full cash payment, and an acceptance was received a few days later. Deeds were drawn up and, after some weeks of back and forth communication with the solicitor managing the dispersal of the estate, not long after his thirtieth birthday Seán O'Dowd sold The Mermaid's Purse to another couple, and he took his young family to the far west coast of Ireland, and towards a life of rural bliss.

* * *

It is always a risk to buy *a pig in a poke* – to purchase something not seen, in the hope of a bargain – but when Seán and his family arrived at Cnoc Feirme an Rí[1] – King's Hill Farm – they were far from disappointed.

The farmhouse was big, in beautiful condition and well appointed, and the land was fertile. Although it had gone to seed over the intervening unmanaged seasons, there was good, sweet-smelling, dark earth with green grass, old oats, wild herbs and orchids. The sheep, looked after by a neighbour, were strong, thick-fleeced and had, in the spring, produced a good number of lambs.

A lark took to the cool spring sky and sang, high in the blue, as Seán walked up the slope to the top of the highest field. Cresting the cliff-top, the strong Atlantic breeze swept over him, bringing the smell of salt, a misting of spray and the promise of new and bright tomorrows. Standing where the turf spilled over the edge of the land, like foam on a wave, the publican-turned-farmer gazed over endless miles of shark-grey rolling ocean to where the horizon poured over the edge of the world. He marvelled at the expanse of water, stretching to infinity in all directions from his vantage point, and wondered what lay beneath its opaque surface and thought about the lands of promise, far to the west.

---

[1] Cnoc Feirme an Rí – pronounced 'K'nock Ferm an Ree'

Later, Seán picked his way down the cliffs, along a path that looked like it had been foot-smoothed for centuries: carved by sheep hooves, and polished by rabbits' soft paws. He strode proudly along the shoreline – *his* shoreline – listening to the water rattling and sucking at the pebbles, and skimmed flat stones, between the waves.

As the sun began to sink, and Seán had all but toured the entirety of his new kingdom while Aoife made the home cosy for them all, he came to one final field: It was at the edge of the land he owned and had been left for grazing, with close-cropped spongy grass, surrounded by a grey, lichen-spattered dry stone wall. There were no sheep here at present, and Seán's attention was taken solely by the centre of the field, where a large mound, twice the height of a man, was surrounded by twisted hawthorn trees.

This was clearly a sídhe[2] – a fairy mound – where, if the old stories were to be believed, the Tuatha Dé Danann, the ancient fay race of Ireland, agreed to retreat to after their defeat, and was the entrance to where they now dwelled.

Mostly, the mound was unremarkable and like many others of its type he'd seen on his journey through the countryside of Ireland, on the way to his new home. Stepping inside the ring of hawthorns, with their tough green leaves and the first hints of blossom in their buds, he strolled around the base of the mound, chuckling at the foolish folk tales of how people would be drawn into these mounds and taken off to the land of the fairies, never to be seen again.

And then he found a hole.

There weren't many rabbits in the centre of Dublin and the books he'd been reading on agriculture hadn't covered off points about wildlife, but at almost a yard at its widest point, he reckoned it was *probably* a rabbit hole, maybe a badger or a fox – now that *was*

---

[2] Sídhe – pronounced similarly to 'she'

something he'd have to look out for at lambing time. He knelt down and peered into the gloom but couldn't see very far, and the entrance was curtained with cobwebs, suggesting it hadn't been used in a while.

Maybe it was that the sun had dropped and, down at the foot of the fields that sloped up to the cliff, there were afternoon shadows on this early spring day, or maybe it was something at the back of his mind telling him that there was always some truth in the old stories; either way, with a supressed shiver, he thought it was time he was getting back to the house.

Standing and brushing the earth off his knees he headed back to his new home, but not without a few glances behind at the fairy mound, although he couldn't have explained why.

* * *

When he reached the house it was almost dark. It was a fine building of grey stone with a wide wooden veranda, either side of the front door that he looked forward to using in the summer, and he imagined himself sitting with his wife, watching the sheep and drinking a glass of beer and smoking his pipe as their children played, unfettered, on the grass. Proprietorially he stepped up, onto the veranda to survey his kingdom, remembering the name of the property, Cnoc Feirme an Rí – King's Hill Farm – and, in that moment he did, indeed, feel like the king of his own little land.

And then he found the bell.

It looked like an old ship's bell, used for ringing out the time or to rouse the crew in case of emergency. It had no clapper, but was otherwise very like the bell he had had behind the bar at The Mermaid's Purse. Judging by the ancient and weatherworn barnacles that dotted its surface in places, this one had spent some time at the bottom of the sea. Smiling, and feeling like he was greeting an old friend, he unhooked the bell from the cast-iron bracket it hung from, and took it indoors to clean it up by the fireside, that evening.

That night, the O'Dowd family ate a good meal, cooked on a good stove, glowing with smouldering slabs of peat, in a warm and cosy house, and slept long and deep in the beds of their new home at King's Hill Farm.

* * *

The next day Seán went into the local town to find people to help get the farm working again and enquire about a workhorse. With the money he'd made from the sale of the pub and the cheap price he'd paid for the farm, he still had quite a bit left over. Horses were expensive and it might have been cheaper to borrow one from a neighbouring farm, but he felt that someone of his newly acquired gentleman farmer status should have his very own horse – and, besides, buying a horse out here in the country was bound to be cheaper than in the middle of Dublin.

Unfamiliar with the town and wanting to find a reliable source of good information, he did what *was* familiar and headed straight to a pub that looked in good shape, to see what he could find out.

An Cat Dubh[3] – The Black Cat – was well built and in good repair, clean and, at this time of day quiet. Thick, greyed oak beams, originally from ships that had been broken up for their timbers after their useful lives had ended, spanned and propped up the ceiling of the bar room, their age revealed by the use of wooden pegs to join them rather than iron nails. A few regulars nursed pints around the edges of the room while a rangy man sat on a stool at the bar plucking absently at an Irish-style, flat-backed and teardrop-shaped mandolin.

---

[3] An Cat Dubh – pronounced 'An Cat Dooh'v

Stepping up and ordering a pint, Seán said a good morning to the musician, who returned his greeting and remarked that they didn't often get people travelling through, this near to the end of the world, and enquired as to his destination.

"*This* is my destination", replied Seán, beaming. "I've come with my wife and children to live here. We've bought a farm and I'm here to hire hands to help me".

"There's plenty of people looking for work, hereabouts", replied the musician. "But I'm not aware of any farm that needs help. Where is it that you've moved to?"

"I am the proud new owner of Cnoc Feirme an Rí", said Seán, beaming again, anticipating a warm response.

Instead, the musician's face fell. His eyes widened and his mouth opened. "Where?" he whispered.

"Cnoc Feirme an Rí", repeated Seán. "King's Hill Farm", he said in English, just in case there was some misunderstanding.

"I know Cnoc Feirme an Rí. Everyone who was born here knows Cnoc Feirme an Rí, but no one has worked on that farm for decades".

"Nonsense", replied Seán. "Sure, the land's gone to seed, but it's only been a year".

"No. No *person* has farmed that land for *decades*". Now the musician looked about before leaning in, his voice almost a whisper. "The man who owned that cursed land before you summoned *something ... things* to do the labouring for him".

Seán wrinkled his nose in amused disbelief, but this just seemed to inflame the musician's fear, "Have you seen the mound in the far field? *That* is the King's hill".

For reasons he couldn't account for, bringing that old hummock into conversation made Seán uncomfortable and he thought of the rabbit hole in its side.

"The King that lies beneath that hill was put there long before God came to Ireland, back in the days of the Great Kings. The old bards tell histories of how he was a tyrant who claimed dominion over everything he could see from the cliff top – both land and ocean – and how everyone within that sight was his to command. He was such a cruel and ruthless ruler who coveted his land and his gold, and bled his subjects for his pleasures, that his people buried him alive and the pagan priests muttered spells over his tomb to *keep* him alive so that he could atone for his crimes for eternity".

Seán scoffed at this nonsense but, still, he felt uneasy. He opened his mouth to say how such things were just old wives' tales but the musician continued unabated. "Strange things happened up at that farm. The old farmer was often seen sitting on the side of the mound, talking out loud, but there was no one there to listen – at least, no one you could see; and the bell – just like that one", he pointed to the bell hanging behind the bar. "When the old farmer rang the bell the mists would come in, and in the mists came *things* – terrible things, unholy things", the man finished, crossing himself.

"Now stop", said Seán, bringing up his hands and laughing away the bumpkin nonsense. "I don't believe in fairies, I don't believe in leprechauns or ghosts or whatever it is that your trying to frighten me with. I've moved into King's Hill Farm and I'm looking for men to help me farm it, in return for an honest wage".

"You'll not find any honest man to work for your honest wage on that farm", advised the musician. "Good luck to you finding anyone to help at all".

And with that, he drained his drink, shook Seán's hand with sincere concern as he stood there, not knowing how to answer this revelation, and then swept out of the pub, calling over his shoulder as he departed, "And, for God's sake, don't ring that bloody bell".

* * *

Despite thinking him clearly mad, the rest of that morning revealed the mandolin player's opinion to be anything other than unique: the other men he spoke to in that pub and many others all wanted nothing to do with King's Hill Farm.

Furious at what he saw as ill-educated, rural ignorance and superstition, Seán asked the advice of the man he was buying a workhorse from, who'd moved to that area a few years ago and didn't hold much stock in the stories of King's Hill Farm.

He was a big man, strong, and slow and steady in his way of being, like the great Shire horses he sold, "I know two lads who'll work for you. They're not clever and they'll need watching, as they can be lazy, but they know how to work the land and it's late for you to plough and plant, but you should still have time. They do some work for me sometimes, but I don't have enough for them at the moment and they'll be glad of the extra money. I'll send them over to you tomorrow, so look out for them".

Seán thanked the man and after they'd spat on their palms and shaken hands to seal the sale of the animal, the horse trader said to come back tomorrow and he'd have had the farrier put a set of new shoes on the beast.

Feeling heartened by his last meeting Seán bought a pie for his lunch and then turned home.

* * *

Arriving back at his farm, Seán went to see how his wife was getting on. She was baking, and a wonderful homely smell of fresh bread filled the house. She smiled and they enjoyed a hug, while the children ran up and joined in.

He felt about as far away as it was possible to be from pagan kings and curses and fairy mounds when he stepped out to do his afternoon rounds. Hanging the old bell, now free from barnacles, back on its bracket outside the door, he laughed at the idea that there was something ghostly about the farm and to prove it to himself and to the world, he picked up a hammer and rang a single, clear note, that seemed to carry across the land and across the sea and further.

* * *

Seán did his rounds, checking walls and fences, counting the small flock of twenty seven sheep, peacefully grazing and dotted across the field that lead up to the cliff edge. When he got to the small field that was farthest from the farmhouse, the one with the fairy mound at its centre, he decided it was getting late and he didn't need to check it at the moment, as the sheep were fenced off elsewhere. Instead, he'd reward himself with an early evening – this farming business wasn't half as hard as people made it out to be.

As he had time he walked back along the cliff top, breathing in deep draughts of sea air. The setting sun had turned the western horizon to a deep, arrestingly beautiful, bloody red, shot through with gold; and what was that in the distance – sea fog? Well, that was just the sort of thing that happened when you lived by the ocean and nothing to worry about.

Pulling his coat tight around him, Seán walked the rest of the way back to the farmhouse, perhaps a little quicker than he would have liked to admit.

* * *

Night passed with strange dreams of deep-tolling bells, of black, silent water and the glimmer of gold in cold, suffocating earth.

In the morning, Seán was not quick to rise and do his rounds, especially seeing as the sheep would look after themselves for a while and he didn't need to collect the horse until the afternoon.

When he finally did rise he dawdled over his breakfast of thick-fatted bacon and the soft white bread Aoife had made the night before, but eventually pulled on his boots and strode out into the fresh, early spring air.

Taking in a deep breath he noticed an odd and unpleasant scent on the air – something wet, salty and fishy – and followed his nose to the source.

In one of the fields used for oats, in a corner was a long mound of seaweed, glistening in the morning light and making quiet hissing and popping noises as it dried and settled in the sunshine. A dreadful sense of horror started to creep over Seán, but then he suddenly remembered – seaweed: very good fertiliser for soil. Those lads the horse trader recommended must have brought up a load and dropped it off – he'd thank the man when he saw him later, for recommending such good workers.

Counting the sheep was more of a challenge.

No matter how many times he did it, he could only account for twenty six. He checked the fences, but they were secure, there was no wool in the field to show a wild dog or even a fox had attacked one. He even peered over the edge of the cliff just to make sure one hadn't gone over, but there was no sign. He must have miscounted the day before.

* * *

In town, later that day, the horse trader seemed surprised that the lads he'd suggested had been over so quickly, but was pleased for Seán and said he'd ask them to go by again that afternoon or tomorrow morning to help with the ploughing. For the second time in as many days, Seán left town feeling happy and satisfied, this time riding bareback on the big, fearless Shire horse that was going to pull the heavy plough that was in the barn, so he could sow his crop of oats.

* * *

That evening, after a lot of hard but rewarding work, his redoubtable horse, it's mighty shoulder higher than his own, was now safely bedded down in the barn in its stall, gated with thick wooden beams and the strong, braced oak planks in the barn walls would keep any foul or cold weather on the outside. Wedging a bucket of water in one corner and hanging a net bag of hay from a nail, Seán fussed the big animal's soft nose, thinking that he must choose a suitable name for the impressive beast, before checking on the tack and harness he had ready to fit that day, if the lads arrived, or tomorrow morning if they didn't, ready for ploughing the fields, ready for sowing.

A check of the fields and boundaries brought him to the strange, lonely field with the sídhe – the fairy mound – which had an odd, cold dampness hanging in the air. He walked the boundaries, which wasn't really necessary, seeing as the dry stone walls had been there for decades if not centuries, but he wanted to prove something to himself: that a field and a pile of earth and old fairy tales didn't worry him.

He even went and peered at the hole. The cobwebs were gone, presumably cleared by some animal passing through the entrance, and the fresh earth sprayed from the opening in an outward direction must also be the work of an animal. Well, it was spring and rabbits had probably taken up residence in the old tunnels, ready to have their babies. He'd have to see to that – get a man with some ferrets d a long dog down here to clear them out before they settled in to ɪake a family and ate his young crop as it emerged from the ɟround – he'd read about that somewhere.

Yes. Rabbits. Definitely. Definitely rabbits.

After checking his sheep – and yes, there were twenty six – Seán decided that it was time to take the advice of the neighbour who'd looked after them while the farm was waiting for a new owner, and get them shorn to sell their winter fleeces before they started to drop off by themselves or become too muddied and tangled with briars and lose any value they might have had. So, in the afternoon he walked over to visit his neighbour who agreed to help drive Seán's flock over to his place where the sheerer was visiting, and Seán would see him right in return – that's what you did in farming, it seemed, you helped each other out for everyone's mutual benefit. Always 'a businessman and not a fighter', this suited Seán perfectly and he rubbed his hands in anticipation of the first income from his new, agricultural venture.

Another successful day came to a close and after a quick check on the sheep Seán headed home to be greeted by his children running and jumping into his arms. Aoife stood at the farmhouse door, wiping her hands on her pinny, smiling, and completing the vision of rural and domestic bliss.

As they all entered the farmhouse for the night he paused outside. Making a great show of it for his family, he rang time on the bell, just like he used to in the old pub, in Dublin, feeling the sound cut the air and rush away in all directions.

The door to the farmhouse closed, leaving the clear, sonorous note of the bell decaying slowly to silence as evening pulled on its coat of shadows.

* * *

For the second night in a row, sleep brought dark and unsettling dreams. Seán heard the sucking, bubbling sound of water and the susurration of stones sliding over each other, and was then surrounded by, crushed by, moving bodies – people, but people he dared not look at. They shuffled silently around him, in an obscuring twilight, brushing their cold, wet bodies against him while something ancient and terrible watched over everything, claiming dominion over everything – everything it could see across the land and across the waves – but the thing itself was always just out of sight. He heard animals screaming, terror and death in their throats and smelled the warm, ferrous scent of blood as the silent people took an unholy sacrament, before the dream descended into a chaotic, thundering, bubbling darkness.

Then silence and waking.

Seán found it difficult to get up that morning, but get up he did. Stumbling around the kitchen, Aoife asked after his health and, kindly, he dismissed her concerns as just the result of a bad night's sleep.

Doorstep sandwich in hand he stepped out and into the chill, early spring air – there was that smell again: Wet, salty and something close to fishy. He went back to the field to see if there had been another delivery of seaweed, like yesterday, but what he saw made him stop, stock still, mouth open, sandwich forgotten in his hand.

There was no seaweed to be seen.

There was no seaweed to be seen, because it had all been ploughed into the field. From where he stood at the gate, line after line of perfectly ploughed furrows and ridges ran away from him in a vanishing perspective to the opposite end of the fields. Beautifully turned dark earth lay open to the sky and crows and gulls marched up and down, pecking at exposed insects and worms.

Running to the barn, past his other crop fields that were also ploughed and lined, he found the doors closed and barred as he'd left them. Sliding the wooden bar out of its brackets and throwing it aside in his hurry, Seán entered the fusty gloom, only to find a gaping hole in the wall at the back of his new horse's stall and the horse itself, a very large and very powerful animal, was nowhere to be seen.

On investigation, the beams that made the sliding gate for the horse's stall were in place and didn't seem to have been moved, but it was clear that the horse had kicked out a number of planks from the wall, despite their robust fixings. The animal's harness, tack and collar also seemed to be undisturbed so, for Seán, that seemed to rule out someone trying to steal the horse, so something must have spooked it to have made it make such a dramatic and terrified escape.

Hurrying back towards to the doors to look for his runaway horse, Seán happened to glance at the plough that was stored in the barn. Whereas, the day before, the ploughshares had been gleaming white metal, this morning they were caked with muddy, dark earth.

The fields had been ploughed – ploughed with *this* plough – but without his horse, which had run away. He was starting to wonder if there was some truth to the stories about fairies – or whatever they were.

A brief inspection of the ground near the newly ploughed fields showed signs of tracks: boot prints in the soft earth and something else, something scratching, almost like claws – perhaps dogs, but no, too long and too deep. Following the tracks, Seán found they came from and went back to the cliff edge, to where the rough little path zigzagged down the cliff face, back to the beach, and yes, there were clods of dark, muddy soil here and there. Whoever had ploughed the field – and, presumably, had also brought the seaweed the night before – had come this way, gaining access and exiting via the beach.

After finding his horse, several fields away, putting a halter on it, leading it back and tethering it in another part of the barn he told Aoife what had happened. She inspected the field, the barn, the tack, the horse and the plough, and they decided that the only sensible explanation was that those farm hands must have ploughed the field yesterday afternoon and they'd missed them and, later, the horse had been spooked … by something.

Still, it was very strange, but there was nothing to be done, but for Seán to repair the barn wall before his neighbour arrived to help drive his sheep over to his farm for shearing. But now, here was another strange thing: There were only twenty five sheep. Several counts and several recounts and checking the walls and the cliff gave no more clues – there were definitely only twenty five sheep.

It didn't take long with the help of his neighbour's dogs to round up the flock and drive them through the fields, along a couple of miles of lanes and into the neighbour's barn, ready for shearing the next day, so Seán decided to go home, via town to see if he could find these two lads who'd been working so hard for him.

In the trader's yard, a large bay horse was tethered to an iron ring, fixed on the outside of a stable wall. While the trader looked on, two young men were grooming the animal's brown flanks and black mane and tail. The big man greeted Seán warmly and introduced him to the young men. He shook them both by the hands with much thanks and enthusiasm, but their faces were clouded with confusion: No, they hadn't done any work for Seán and no, they hadn't been to King's Hill Farm either and, especially after what Seán had to say, would they go there at all!

Who had done the work, they weren't willing to speculate, but instead hurriedly left with dark glances over their shoulders.

Confused and feeling somewhat deflated Seán spent the walk home wondering who or what were the wonderful benefactors who'd been tending to his farm, without complaint or request for payment.

At the farmhouse door he paused, turning his back to the building and surveying his land, the wet smell no longer in the air, and he came to a decision: He would ring the damned bell and then he would stay up all night if he needed to, to see who came and worked the land. It was, after all, his land and, helpful though they were, he had a right to know!

With a defiant swing of his arm, Seán struck the bell, hard, the clarity and sharpness of the sound hurting his ears before dying away, as if carried to infinity in all directions: into the sky above him, into earth under his feet and into the deeps of the ocean.

Standing for a moment longer after the silence began to sink oppressively onto him, he nodded to himself and turned inside, ready for the night to begin.

* * *

Aoife, had gone to bed one or two hours earlier and the children had been asleep for a long time – everyone was tucked up and cosy, safe and sound in their beds. Meanwhile, Seán had stayed up, sitting in the kitchen. All the lamps were out and the only light was the dim red glow from the banked up fire, glowering in the kitchen range. To keep himself awake Seán paced the room, or smoked a pipe when he was sat in a chair, often parting the curtains, just a crack, to peep out – he was sure he'd see he the lanterns of anyone coming in the night onto his land, creeping up the cliff path.

Minutes ticked by and became hours, and the darkness and the silence seemed to deepen. As many of us do, in the depths of the night, Seán began to become afraid of things he never thought he'd believe in.

What was it that mad musician had said in the pub? A cruel heathen king, buried alive under the mound and cursed by pagan priests; inhuman 'things' that worked the land; magical sea fog that was summoned by the ringing of the bell … the bell he'd rung everyday for the last three days, when he had seen sea mists, and his land had been worked and no one knew by whom.

A spit and a crackle from the fire in the range brought him to full wakefulness, from a doze he hadn't realised he'd slipped into; but something inside him made him feel he had to check to see who – or what – might be outside.

Putting his now cold pipe onto a table, in the orange gloom of the kitchen he crept to the window and, with trembling hands, squeezed the curtains apart, the width of his pupil, to peep out, holding onto the woven cloth like an infant, peering from behind its mother's skirts.

Outside the night was black – black as anger, black as fear – the sky studded with tiny sparkling gemstones, coldly twinkling and twitching but bringing no comfort. Pivoting his body to sweep his viewpoint from side to side and straining his eyes and ears to catch a sign of something – anything – he saw a glow.

From the direction of the coastal path, a dim, shimmering, sickly-green fairy fire was starting to show. As Seán watched, one after another, the silhouettes of shambling, stooping figures breached the cliff top. Their shapes indistinct, but loathsome and terrifying in their awkward movements, more than a score of figures walked, hobbled and stumbled past the farmhouse in absolute and unified silent purpose, the glow seemingly emanating from the figures themselves. He stared, transfixed with fear, still clinging to the curtains, as the group congregated in a nearby field, standing stiller than anything living he knew of could ever stand.

As he watched, another figure joined the throng. Lit by the unholy glow, the new figure seemed taller, straighter, somehow more impressive; cloaked and concealed in long, flowing garments or robes from head to toe, Seán couldn't make out any detail of the new figure, other than what he realised was the glint from a conspicuous, deep band of gold around the entity's head, much like a crown. In silent concert the group knelt before the crowned figure, then rose and headed towards the barn – *his* barn.

A few moments later he heard the panicked whinnying of his horse and a thump … thump … thump, along with the sound of splintering wood, then silence again. Now, there was no way Seán was going outside while those whatever-they-weres were abroad, and at the same time he couldn't leave his window outpost.

In the middle of his wonderment, the group appeared again. Preceded by the chilling, green glow, they came into view, their outlines ragged and tattered, their movements jerky and painful, but carrying what looked like the sacks of seed oats he had stored, ready for planting. Impossibly, each figure that carried a sack seemed to do so with ease, under one arm, something no normal man could do, especially not ones as thin, as emaciated as these. Bringing up the rear two figures carried his harrow: one at the front, one at the back. Again, there was no way two normal men could carry such a heavy piece of farming equipment between them – it normally took a large and strong horse to drag the harrow across a field to smooth the ground after ploughing or planting, but here it was, being carried along like two men might carry a new front door for a house. The procession reminded Seán of Bible stories of slaves building great temples or pulling the chariots of dark-hearted Pharaohs.

The grisly team continued on its way towards the fields that had been ploughed the day before and Seán realised that they were going to sow the crop of oats. After they had disappeared from sight he went back to sit in his chair and think on what to do.

He wasn't going to follow them and, after all, they were actually doing him a favour and working for free, or at least not requiring any sort of payment he could understand – something that appealed strongly to the businessman within him. But he also felt he might need to protect his family from these intruders who had, without invitation or request, marched onto his land and taken it into their own hands to work his farm.

He sat back in his armchair, fretting with indecision as the minutes ticked by, until anxiety and exhaustion got the better of him and he nodded off.

But his sleep was neither refreshing nor long-lived as he was jerked awake by a slow but insistent thumping on his front door. Thinking of his little family upstairs he grabbed a long carving knife from a drawer in the dresser, took a deep breath and threw open the front door, holding the knife up in front of him.

He gasped and almost dropped the blade as, standing outside, lit by the diabolical red glow of the range behind him, was a tall and angular figure, covered head-to-toe in robes that concealed their owner's face and body and pooled on the floor at their feet, while long voluminous sleeves covered its hands. Perhaps the cloth had once been white, but now it was a muddy brown with large, round patches of mould blossoming here and there. A smell like the sweetness of newly dug earth floated off the creature and the cloth covering its head and face was encircled, around the brow, by a deep band of shining gold, but was otherwise plain of features or ornamentation. In the starlit darkness, some way behind the imposing spectre, Seán could make out the shady silhouettes of those who had been to sow his fields. Their oddly posed outlines, etched in their green glow against the darkness, were disconcerting, but it was the way they were absolutely still – no shifting or fidgeting, or movement of any kind – that made them even more eerie.

And then the grand and terrible figure spoke and its voice was like the thunder of falling stones and seemed to echo from a place far away from our existence, "I was once King here, and still hold dominion over those under the land and under the sea within site of my cliffs. As you are the new King of the land above you must honour the bargain struck with the King before you: At the ringing of the bell I will rise from the prison from which your predecessor freed me, and I shall summon my subjects – those who lie beneath the land and beneath the sea – and I shall compel them to work this land, in return for the warm life blood of a beast, to sustain their hungry souls. Tonight, at your ringing, I have come and called them, and they have toiled at my bidding, but there is no beast to bleed".

Of course – the sheep: Dwindling in number after each night the dead King and his subjects had worked the land, but now they were gone and the horse escaped, so there were no 'beasts' for them to find!

"If there is no beast to bleed I will take the blood of those debtors for whom my servants have worked…".

"You will not!" roared Seán, interrupting the wraith, fear and anger overcoming his terror, and thrusting the carving knife into the centre of the King's body.

It felt like cutting through a sack of tightly packed sawdust, then a biting, cramping pain shot up Seán's arm and he snatched his hand away as if he'd been burnt. Looking at the knife, protruding from the rotting robes, frost and ice crystals crackled and furred on the handle and what could be seen of the blade until, with a sound like a whip crack, the metal shattered and its splinters and the stub of the handle dropped to the floor.

The spectre looked down at the fragments, dipping it's veiled, crowned head for a moment, before lifting it again to look at Seán … and then stepped forward. It made as if to enter the house to reach the man, but some unseen force blocked it at the threshold. For a few moments, in a silence only broken by the quiet hiss of the peat, smouldering in the range, the cowled figure turned its head questioningly, inspecting the frame of the doorway before stepping back again.

"As the old King to the new King of this land, I give you one night's grace. I shall return again tomorrow at nightfall to collect the debt … one way or another".

With a sound like the grinding of a millstone, the dead King turned on the spot and swept into the darkness, the horde of shambling followers dispersing towards the cliff top, their sickly phosphorescence dimming as, one by one, they descended the little path, heading back to wherever they came from.

And then they had all gone, and the night was empty once more and a thousand million bright pinpricks of stars were the only things in the darkness.

Seán felt his shoulders soften and drop and he gave a great sigh of relief, but turning and shutting the door behind him, he jumped, with a start of surprise. Aoife was crouched on the stairs, her eyes round with fear and horror. Woken by the knocking on the door, yes, she had seen and heard all that had happened.

Holding each other, Seán trembling from a mixture of fear and rage, they both agreed – something had to be done; done for the sake of their little family, for sake of their home; for the sake of their lives.

* * *

Next morning, his head thick with lack of sleep, when Seán stepped into the light morning drizzle and the cold, bright spring air, he smelled the smell of the sea again, and this time its scent filled him with horror and he felt goose bumps prickle his skin. As he passed fields that had been ploughed and sowed and harrowed by the cold hands of the dead King's men he shuddered and did not look at the scarecrows that now dotted the land, standing at crooked angles, their heads slumped on their chests, arms outstretched in cruciform, and in rags and tatters and some with strands of deep water seaweed blowing like gaunt ribbons in the breeze.

* * *

Seán stepped through the door of the pub, An Cat Dubh, not long
after it had opened. His eyes took a moment to adjust to the gloom,
but he was pleased to see the mandolin player at the bar, in the act
of receiving his first pint of the day, as a penitent receives com-
munion. Curiously he noticed how the man picked up the glass
using both, shaking hands and drained its contents straight down,
and was immediately presented with another, which he just took a
quick sip from, and placed back on the bar – this looked like a daily
ritual.

Used to dealing with troublesome patrons, from his days as the
landlord of The Mermaids Purse, with a grim, determined smile,
Seán purposefully strode up to the man who, hearing his strident
footsteps turned to see who was approaching in such a thunderous
way. Seán's face was grim and, remembering the content of their
last conversation, the musician's eyes opened wide in alarm and he
stepped off his stool, backing away, as Seán bore down on him.

Stopping short, at the bar, watched by the timid, gangly youth who
was serving, Seán put his finger up into the musician's terrified
face and barked one word "Listen!"

Mutely the mandolin player nodded and everyone in the pub froze,
waiting to see what was going to happen.

"I'm a businessman, not a fighter, but fight I will when needs be to
protect my family and my property and now fight I must – and
against *you* know what – and *you* are going to tell me how to defeat
it".

* * *

The place where the mandolin player lived was mean lodgings
above a leather worker's shop and the smell from the materials
used to tan and glue drifted up through the bare floorboards and

filled the one-room garret with a pervasive stench hanging like an almost tangible cloud of gloom. At the man's invitation Seán sat gingerly on the edge of the rickety cot and watched, as he used a folding knife to lever up a floorboard and remove an object, a foot in length and wrapped in a cloth, darkened with dried mud.

Reverentially the musician knelt in front of Seán and, with outstretched arms, carefully peeled back the layers of wrappings. Seán gasped and leaned in, as bright, white metal sparkled in the dim light. Lying across the man's hands was a spearhead, twelve inches long and made of solid silver, but instead of a traditional leaf-shaped blade it was a single point with layers of backward-facing barbs, sweeping down its length, to where the whole piece would be attached to a wooden haft. Even though spears hadn't been used in Ireland for a very long time, this was an ancient style, like something out of a legend, something that the great Irish hero Cúchullain[4] might once have wielded: a devastating gáe bulg[5] - the death spear.

"Not long before the King was first unearthed, this was found on the land, ploughed from the earth and brought out under the sky once more. The King had been released, centuries after his imprisonment, his life sustained by old magic and the venom of his anger, he is still bound by the curses laid upon him, never to leave his Kingdom and unable to pass a threshold without the permission of the owner. He was, and is, afraid of no man and no weapon, save this. It was believed that this spearhead was forged at the time of the King's interment and still posses some of the pagan magic that held him there and, should the need arise, this would be the weapon to defeat him. It now seems that time has come and you have need of this", finished the musician, stretched his arms and offered Seán the spearhead.

---

[4] Cúchullain – pronounced coo-CHULL-uhn, with a soft 'ch', as in 'loch'
[5] Gáe bulg – pronounced 'guy boolg' and variously translated as spear of mortal pain, death spear or belly spear

Quietly taking the shining, marvelous object, Seán asked, "How do you know all of this? How come you have … *this*?"

"My name is Brendan McCaul, son of John McCaul, who was the last owner of Cnoc Feirme an Rí – King's Hill Farm. It was my father who raised the King from his tomb and struck a bargain with him and his unholy subjects to do the work of a hundred men in return for the blood of a lamb."

"Your father? Now I see how you know so much. But with the money from the sale of the farm, why do you live like … like this", Seán gestured round the filthy, reeking room.

"I have to keep moving. I fear that the King will come after me someday, somehow. I move quarters ever few weeks", and for the second time, Seán noticed a trembling in the Jack's hands.

"If you take the spearhead and slay the King", Jack continued, "I will move away – maybe go across the sea to England and live in peace at last and you can run the farm in peace without the need for that unholy revenant".

Seán nodded. "I'm a businessman, not a fighter, but fight I will if the need is there", and solemnly he took the ancient, solid silver spearhead from the weary man.

* * *

Night had fallen many hours before, the death of twilight marked by the ringing of the summoning bell. The children, Fia and Colm, had been put to bed with as much normality as their parents could muster, to hide the dreadful truth from their innocent offspring, but within an hour of them dozing off, Aoife had gently scooped them up and now sat, huddled with them, in her own bed, their little sleeping forms soft and warm, while Seán prepared for the night ahead.

Deep in bowels of the night, at that time so deep that the silence of the night hangs like a weight upon the roofs of farms and lintels of doorways, that perfect fearful quiet was cracked wide open by three slow hammerings on the wooden door of the farmhouse.

As ready as he ever would be, Seán still jumped at the sound and then ran his hands along the ash handle upon which he'd mounted the ancient, silver spearhead. Taking a deep breath and steeling himself to the task ahead he stood, walked to the door and, with a determined hand, pulled it open.

Filling the doorframe was the silent King, the musty ancient shroud covering him from the top of his head, down his body, gathering at his feet and drifting faintly in a breeze Seán couldn't feel, the ancient crown a shining gold band encircling his faceless brow. He could see the slit in the robe, where he had plunged the carving knife into the unresponsive body, the night before.

Some distance behind the dread figure, cloaked in their dim, green glow, stood the ranks of the dead who had come at the King's call, their outlines indistinct and unnaturally still.

When the King spoke, his voice came, as if from deep caverns far below the earth's surface, echoing, and rasping like the wind through reeds, "I have come for payment owed to me and my subjects". At these last words, the spectre lifted an arm and began to reach out for Seán who, remembering last night's meeting and what Jack had said, took a small step back into the safety of his home, behind the threshold the King could not cross.

"If you deny me, and hide behind your doorway, I shall have my subjects tear down your house so that no portal stands against us", the King was about to continue when Seán brought the silver-headed spear into full view and this time it was the King's turn to take a step backward and the grim ranks behind him shifted and seemed to stand more to attention.

"I see you have armed yourself", hissed the King, passing one covered hand into the sleeve of the other arm and producing a verdigrised blade as long as a man's shin. "If a fight is what you want I will happily grant that wish and let us see who has the greater skill".

But Seán, not moving from behind the protection of the door and the power it had over the dead King planted the butt of spear on the floor and raised his hand. "I am a businessman and not a fighter, but fight I will when the need arises. However … if there is no real need, then a businessman I'll stay".

Standing to one side he gave a clear view from where the King stood, to the interior of the farmhouse. Tied to the leg of a sturdy piece of furniture was a lamb.

"Now, if you keep to your side of the bargain and bring … men … to work on my land in a way that no living man could possibly achieve, and in return I provide an animal I had already raised for slaughter, I can see no harm in continuing the arrangement. When I ring the bell, you will bring your subjects and I will provide payment, and in the in-between-times you will keep the dead from my land. My farm will benefit – and as a result so shall I – and you may keep your dominion over your subjects lost under the earth or out at sea, and walk abroad those nights the bell is rung. Alternatively, we can finish this here and now, or tomorrow my neighbour will hurl that bloody bell into the sea, as I've asked him to if I don't call on him, where it'll never be rung again. What do you think?"

The King was silent for a moment, his sword arm slowly descending, and then spoke again, "It seems we have renewed the bargain. As you shall be 'King Over the Land' where once I was, I shall also be 'King Under the Land and Waves.

Seán nodded, released the animal's tethering, tossing the end of the rope to the King who turned and walked towards the line of dead. Seán quietly, but firmly closed the door on the dead King's receding form, sliding home both bolts – just in case – before running upstairs to hold his wife and children and both tried to ignore the noises outside.

* * *

King's Hill Farm continued to prosper over the years, it's owner, one Seán O' Dowd, previously a publican from Dublin ran it well. As those who knew the history of the farm and it's original resident slipped away it became understood that Seán and his son employed the help of itinerant gypsies who appeared at certain times of the year to work the fields, to sow and, later to gather the harvest of grain. The flock of sheep the farmer kept were mainly used for meat for the family and the visiting workers and only on very good years was there enough to send to market.

The farm was handed down from father to son, but when Seán's son, who had never married, died, the farm was sold to an incomer to the area who was keen to start using the latest steam engines and machine threshers that had been invented. Curiously none of the gypsies that used to work the farm returned after the son's death, but as part of the covenant that came with the house, the new owner followed its instructions, as he was bound to, before any deeds could be handed over and had the local smith melt down an old brass bell that hung outside the farm house, and cast into nine ingots, each of which were dropped into deep water at mile intervals along the coast.

The only oddity about the farm was what the old folk called a fairy mound that had been plundered over a century ago. The new owner hoped that one day an archaeologist might dig it open and they would share in whatever they found inside, in the hope that it wasn't empty.

The Clay Dragon of Staffordshire, England

Everyone has sayings in their family, which seem totally normal to anyone within that family, but often impenetrable to those outside; mine is no exception: A 'Fitzherbert', meaning something that will fit anyone – what 'fits Herbert' will fit you; the 'doofer', something without a name or a name that cannot be recalled in that moment, but rather than just being a 'what's is called' or a 'thingy', a 'doofer' will 'do for this' or 'do for that'.

But there's one in particular I remember clearly, which is to 'go all round the Wrekin': the same as 'all around the houses', describing something that is an excessively long journey, as the Wrekin is a hill in Shropshire that may have to be awkwardly circumnavigated.

The Wrekin is an odd, isolated hill, springing up in otherwise flat countryside and we can pause a moment and indulge ourselves with the folklore that describes how it came into being, before we get onto our own story. There are many versions and variations but the main points are all agreed upon:

> There was once a Welsh giant who held a grudge against the people of the town of Shrewsbury, in Shropshire, over the border in England, and decided to teach them a lesson by flooding the town. To do this he took a huge shovel and scooped up one of the black mountains on the Welsh borderland, digging it up from its roots.

> He then strode over to England and headed towards Shrewsbury, carrying the heavy load, until he met a cobbler coming the other way who asked him where he was going and why he was carrying such an enormous shovelful of earth and rock.

The giant explained that he was off to teach the people of Shrewsbury a lesson by dumping the mountain, that he had on his shovel, into the river Severn near the town and that would drown all the folk of that cursed place.

Hearing this and wanting to save the town and its people, the cobbler, being a canny fellow, like may of his trade, in the folk tales of Britain, sighed and mopped his brow and shook his head.

The giant wanted to know what the matter was and the cobbler, feigning regret, told him that Shrewsbury was so far away. Why, he had worn out any number of shoes, just walking there, himself and to prove it he emptied out the sack of old shoes he was carrying home to mend.

Seeing all the shoes and not relishing the effort of carrying the mountain on the shovel for what seemed a *very* long way, the giant instead gave up and tipped the dug up mountain onto the ground where he was and turned home; that mound of earth become the Wrekin hill.

That such a folk tale endures is charming as there are few today who would believe it, despite its absolute truth. But there is another story, which is no longer told because if the truth were known there would be great risk to many lives, even today.

Less than forty miles from the Wrekin is Newcastle Under Lyme, where my mother was born, in the county of Staffordshire. If you are not familiar with this county of middle England it was, until the industrial revolution, just like many others, full of towns and villages and farms and artisans. But what Staffordshire became really famous for was its potteries, where the likes of Josiah Wedgewood set up headquarters and factories, and produced high quality ceramics on an industrial scale and people moved away from their farms and took up work with some of the most fantastically named jobs in the world, including 'slip house blunger operator', 'glost rubber' and – the finest job title ever known – a 'sagger maker's bottom knocker'.

If you doubt the truth of these job names, you can investigate them yourself but, for instance, a 'sagger maker's bottom knocker' was a low skilled person who worked for someone who made the ceramic stand, or 'sagger', on which ceramics sat when they went into the kiln to be fired. After firing, this low skilled and low paid individual would remove the object from the kiln and strike the sagger, detaching it from the object, leaving only slight marks in the glaze on the underside. Hence one who knocks the sagger off the bottom of the ceramic and works for the one who produces the sagger itself is, quite clearly, a 'sagger maker's bottom knocker'.

Before the potteries came and new towns and cities sprang up across Staffordshire something happened that must remain a secret and I am telling you this in strictest confidence, so you must not tell too many others. That it needed to be a secret, was identified by a predecessor of mine, called Rupert Simms, who was a direct descendant of the person involved. Rupert was also born in Newcastle Under Lyme, but this time, earlier than my mother, in 1830, about one hundred and fifty years after the actual event took place.

If you choose to investigate Rupert Simms you will find he is remembered for two things: Firstly, that he is the author of a historical textbook still used for reference today and kept in many libraries the world over, and secondly that he achieved this despite having no hands. He is, in fact, the only recorded person in history to produce a work of literature, despite having no hands.

Today people roll their eyes and moan about 'health and safety gone mad', but at the age of six and visiting his father at work, little Rupert got his arms caught in a brick making machine, losing one hand and his other forearm.

The foreman gave him sixpence for not crying and the limbs were buried in the churchyard.

Unable to learn to write, he was relegated to the back of the class to give priority to pupils who were likely to achieve at school. However, one teacher in particular, took an interest in young Rupert and encouraged him in his studies. Soon the young lad had worked out how to thrust a stylus – used for writing on school slates at the time – into one of the leather purses that covered the stump on his wrist and not only did he actually learn to write, but he himself became a teacher in his teens. Later, he turned his attention to dealing in rare and antique books and ultimately, as a labour of love, produced the definitive history of the county of Staffordshire, 'Biblioteca Staffordiensis'.

Now, while this is a fine, if very dry codex, collecting histories and records of documentation, it is also a cover-up. Whereas this story I am about to tell you has been handed down by word of mouth from parent to child, throughout my family, if you read Rupert Simms' venerable tome you will find no mention whatsoever of the story I am about to tell you, thus proving its veracity.

* * *

People often think of wizards and warlocks as hairy bearded men in flowing robes, confining themselves, in isolation, to caves and towers and muttering into their spell books and porridge as they unravel the mysteries of the multiverse; not so with Avaricious Turnpenny. I'm not sure 'Avaricious Turnpenny' was the man's actual name, but everyone loves a baddie, and this is the name he is known by so this is the name I'm going to call him.

Avaricious Turnpenny had plenty of money but a great hunger for more. With the great wealth he had already accumulated he could afford to pay for tuition from the aforementioned cave or tower-dwelling wizards, for premises within which to practise, the expensive materials required, and had gathered a significantly dangerous working knowledge of magic.

He was a proud man, dressed impeccably in the latest fashions of the time: a silk frock coat with deep, richly embroidered cuffs, shining knee-high riding boots and a snappy beaver felt cocked hat, or tricorne.

But, when he turned up at the farmhouses in Staffordshire, the most remarkable thing about this attire was a tiny, wingless, red clay dragon that clung to his lapel, like a broach. In fact many thought is was a broach, but a few saw the smoke curling from its tiny nostrils and that it occasionally moved and shifted position.

Avaricious pointed out to the farmers how poor the thick clay soil was and how difficult it was to farm and offered not inconsiderable sums to buy their land and everything on it. While some took up his offer, most declined it either because of pride or because they were just unwilling to give up land that had been in their families for generations or offered at least a dependable, if not very profitable, livelihood.

The second time the wealthy wizard visited the farms not only did he offer less money but this time everyone saw the dragon as it was now the size of a cat and lay across his shoulders like a thick collar made of red clay with spikes down its back, curving claws and glowing eyes.

The third time he visited he came riding the dragon, which was now the size of a cow, and would suddenly grab handfuls of the clay soil and toss them into its mouth. Its body was the colour of terracotta, along its back were what looked like ridge tiles from the top of a roof, its tail was like flowerpots stacked inside each other, its limbs like chimney pots, its claws like curved roof finials and while smoke drifted from its nostrils it eyes glowed like coals in a forge.

This time he offered very little money, saying it was his final offer, and that next time he returned he would simply take what he wanted before directing the dragon away, it's body walking with jerky, twitching movements, rattling, with clinking noises like a tea set jiggling and chinking against itself.

The unfortunate farmers and their families didn't know what to do. When they thought of how the dragon was growing they dreaded what would happen next. When they went and sought help from the appropriate authorities they were laughed at for being bumpkins, quaking in their boots at a fairy tale – and some said they thought that Avaricious Turnpenny had got to them first and used either his dragon or his money to make sure nothing was done. So they turned to the only person they knew who had a knowledge of things mystical and magical – Jack Bagnall, Rupert Simms', and my, ancestor.

Now, Jack Bagnall, born Jacqueline de Bagnall, pronounced originally as 'ban-yall', apparently from some distant French ancestors, a young woman with eccentric ways, was what you'd call a hedge witch: No rituals or spells, no grimoires or ceremonies, just the simple understanding and manipulation of natural magic, to call on spirits and elementals, to know which plants to pick and use for poultices and potions and to have the knack of knowing how to reset a dislocated joint or birth a particularly troublesome calf.

The farmers came to her and pleaded with her for her help and after what she felt was a suitable amount of pleading she told them yes, of course she'd help them against the dragon of clay and its master, and to call her when they came again.

Time passed, but when Avaricious Turnpenny arrived again, with the dragon, the beast was so vast that the man was enjoying riding it from the comfort of a small and decorative cabin mounted on its back.

Each of the dragon's tiled and jointed paws were finished with ceramic claws the size of flying buttresses and thick as a man's waist. Its huge body, covered in thousands upon thousands of scales like roof tiles, was the size of a small town, could have accommodated several small farms and you could have driven three carriages, side by side, through its cavernous maw while it's eyes glowed fiercely like pottery kilns. As it moved across the landscape, with Avaricious Turnpenny, leaning out of a window in the cabin, puffing on a long-stemmed churchwarden clay pipe, its body rattled and its baked clay scales clattered musically. It dug its great claws into the thick ground, greedily gulping down tonne after tonne of the rich clay, and hot, freshly fired bricks fell like eggs or like other 'things' that fall from the back ends of animals.

Jack Bagnall had been hurriedly fetched. Now she knew this day would come, but she hadn't prepared for it, but that was the way of the hedge witch, to work on your wits and your instincts. She knew the tales of dragons and how they were magical and very clever, but also very proud. But she'd never actually met a real dragon and when she arrived on the land of the farmer whose farmhouse was being crushed while his land was gouged and eaten, she damn near peed her panickles at the site of the colossal beast as it went about its destruction without a care that she even existed.

Looking at the terrified faces of the hapless farmer and his family she swallowed her own fear and called out…

> *Come sun and moon!*
> *Come night and day!*
> *Hear me Great Dragon!*
> *Of English clay!*

Flattered to be addressed in rhyme, the dragon stopped its destruction and peered down at the tiny woman, its head the size of a church and with eyes that glowed like the fires of a kiln. Again she called up to it, "Oh, great dragon, I have been chosen as the champion for these people and I am here to defeat you!"

Immediately the dragon raised one of his house-sized paws, ready to crush this tiny irritant, but Jack called out quickly, "I have three challenges for you that I'm sure you cannot beat!" and the dragon put its giant, clawed paw back on the ground: Along with treasure, fame and flattery, there are few things dragons like more than winning.

Jack continued, heartened by the dragon's cessation of hostilities. "I challenge you to three challenges: A test of strength, a test of wit and a test of endurance. If I beat you, you will agree to leave this place and never return…", the dragon, of course agreed without any thought of losing and would likely do what it wanted anyway – but it wanted to win and be seen to win. "If you win, you may eat me and continue your domination over this land". Well, thought Jack, it'll do that anyway, but she thought she'd dress it up to make it sound more like a prize.

And it worked. The dragon nodded in agreement. But Avaricious Turnpenny cried out from his cabin on the dragon's back, "What is this nonsense! Continue the demolition, I command you!"

Now, if there's something dragons *don't* like, it's to be commanded – especially by piffling little mortal humans – and, in response to Turnpenny's outcry, it reached up and plucked the cabin on its back and set it on the ground before turning its attention once more to Jack.

"My first challenge is the challenge of strength!" and from a pocket she produced a pouch, filled to bursting with beans. Now, if any of us knows anything about 'Jacks' and their beans, it's that the beans are always magical and these were no exception: Handful after handful she broadcast them up and over the dragon so they fell all around the giant clay reptile. Then, planting her feet firmly on the ground – her ground, the ground of her people – she let the power of nature flow up and into her, and through her, before she sent it back, back down into the earth to reach the beans, making them push out deep roots and sprout long tendrils that crawled up the side of the dragon and criss-crossed its body like a net of green ropes and waving leaves. But the dragon easily pushed its body up and away from the ground, snapping the bean plants like so many thin green strings, and stared imperiously down at the hedge witch.

"Great Dragon! You have bested my test of strength!" she cried up to its towering head, with a sigh that might not have been entirely sincere. "Now, my challenge of wit".

At this, three large oak doors were brought to her, each carried by two men, all of them clearly terrified of the huge clay dragon. They dropped the doors next to each other, on the floor, throwing nervous glances over their shoulders, before scuttling away.

"Oh, Great Dragon, mighty in strength, my next challenge is use your wit to discern which of these doors your mast Avaricious Turnpenny will be hiding behind". At the suggestion of his involvement, the rich man started to puff and bluff and bluster, but the dragon – not liking the idea of having a 'master' picked up the decorative cabin in which Avaricious Turnpenny was still lounging in and shook it like a piggy bank, until the man fell out.

Jack explained that the man was to hide behind one of the doors and the dragon – who must shut its eyes and definitely *not* peep, and who definitely *was* peeping, just so it could make sure it was gong to win – would then choose which doors the man was *not* hiding behind.

After asking it to see if it had made up its mind, Jack gave the last minute instruction to the dragon to slam its paws down on the two doors it thought its master was *not* hiding behind. As the ceramic titan leaned back on its haunches and raised its two forelimbs Jack slipped in a moment of doubt by asking, "Are you sure?"

Distracted and suspecting trickery the dragon brought down just one of its giant paws, slamming it on the remaining door – the one under which Avaricious Turnpenny *was* hiding under and picked the door up to reveal *nothing* on the ground. Of course, if it had turned the door over it would have seen its creator splatted and pressed to the underside of the door like a swatted daddy longlegs, his limbs at unnatural angles and an expression on his face that would have been comical if it hadn't been so gruesome.

Pleased with itself for what it thought of as spotting a deception the dragon slammed its other huge forepaw onto another door and lifted it up with the same result – no Avaricious Turnpenny … it had won the second challenge.

Again, Jack feigned resignation and sighed, "Again, Great Dragon, you have bested me, this time in a challenge of wits. Finally I challenge you to a test of endurance and if you can beat me in this last challenge I will submit to you". If it were possible for a huge reptilian face of fired clay to smile that is what the dragon did, as it shook its head and neck with pleasure and in anticipation of its victory.

"This time", she continued. "I am absolutely confident that I will win and cost you the competition, so, to be fair, I will give you a head start". Here again, the dragon's desire to win overruled any sense of what might really be going on here.

"The challenge of endurance is a competition to see who can remain still for the longest, without moving! You start and when you've had enough of a head start I will join in and we shall see who can last the longest!"

Well … along with treasure, fame, flattery and winning another thing dragons like to do best is lying still for years, even centuries, at a time – preferably on top of piles of their treasure.

So, signalling its agreement the dragon lay down and found a comfortable position in which to lie still. Its huge body, covered in thousands upon thousands of scales like terracotta roof tiles was like a small town on a hill; its long neck and each of its four limbs and tail stretched out like streets of workers' cottages, whilst its great head was like sat in the landscape like a parish church.

Jack watched, making a great show of um'ing and ah'ing, inspecting the dragon's prone form to make sure it wasn't moving.

The minutes ticked by and became hours and Jack still meandered around the static dragon, scrupulously checking it for movement and the dragon lay smugly still. When the sun began to set Jack nodded and made approving noises to the dragon before announcing she would return in the morning to check it hadn't moved.

At dawn the next day she return and was very impressed that the dragon hadn't moved at all and said she would check the next morning as well.

And so it went on, with Jack checking every morning. Then, as the days went passed it became every other day, and then twice a week and then once a week. Days became weeks, became months and the gap between Jack's visits became greater and greater, but each time she made a great fuss of checking to see if the dragon had moved, and was always amazed to see that it hadn't, much to dragon's pleasure. Eventually, as the months turned into years and people didn't just begin to forget that the dragon was a threat, but started to forget it was there, altogether. Farms and lives were rebuilt and the great pits dug by the dragons claws made it possible for people to access the rich clay, and they made their own ceramics that become known far and wide for their excellent quality. During that time Jack also met a man – a blacksmith – and they fell in love and were married and, oh, the children born of the union between a hedge witch and a blacksmith had such power and such wondrous gifts.

Eventually the dragon became more and more of the landscape: People took its scales to use as actual roof tiles, people actually moved into its limbs, like terraced houses in a street; its body – not made of flesh of blood, but magically animated clay and brick – became a thriving town in its own right, and the huge head was used as a church, with a pair of double doors mounted at the entrance to its mouth.

And still the dragon, pleased with its endurance, did not move – it couldn't, lest it forfeit the challenge.

After many years had passed, Jack, now a very old woman visited the dragon one morning. "Well, now", she said. "I think you've proved to me that you've had quite enough of a head start. Tonight I shall lie down and we shall start the challenge in earnest".

That night, surrounded by her family and loved ones, Jack passed away peacefully in her bed. The next morning, she was carried – *lying down* – in her bed to within sight of the dragon's head so that it could see that she was lying still and not moving. Now, as the huge head was being used as the town's church, it seemed perfectly natural for Jack to be buried in the churchyard there – but she'd left strict instructions to be buried in a plot in sight of the dragon, but deeper than the foundations of a cathedral.

And there she lies to this day and so does the dragon.

The town had become known as Ormskirk – not to be confused with the town of the same name in Lancashire, famous for its gingerbread: Ormskirk – Wyrmskirk – or Dragon's Church, in old English.

Woe betide any who might seek out the dragon, or Jack's remains, for to disturb either would be to rouse the mighty beast and who knows what destruction it may leave in its wake.

To prevent this awful occurrence, my ancestor, Rupert Simms, wrote his book, Biblioteca Staffordiensis, and conspicuously omitted the town of Ormskirk. In fact, such an effective cover up was made that no matter where you search, you will never find any reference to the town of Ormskirk in Staffordshire, and by this absence, we know this story to be true.

So please, please, on behalf of the people of Staffordshire and possibly even the whole of England, keep this very true and accurate account of the Clay Dragon of Staffordshire to yourself.

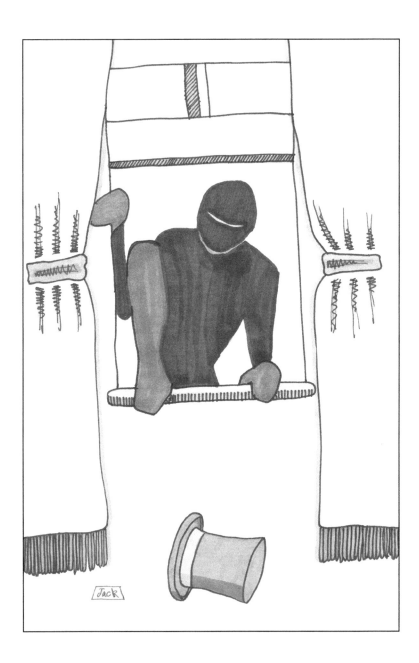

I t was entirely inconceivable to Her Majesty's Constabulary that such a thing could be the case and so, because of their preconceptions and their prejudices, they were oblivious to the facts and that is why she went undetected. In her experience, Millicent Basset found that men were often blind to the most obvious of truths because of these prejudices and whilst most of the time this was an inconvenience, in this instance it was a distinct advantage.

Millicent was the dutiful daughter of Mrs. Jacqueline Basset, lately widowed of the much loved and lamented William 'Jack' Basset. However, whilst approaching a suitably eligible age to marry, she did not relish the idea of becoming the chattel of a man who would tell her to be quiet and submissive, to simper and blush rather than converse and debate, to own her and use her as prize breeding stock for his, and his family's, pride.

Neither her father, a wonderful man who had led her and her mother on expeditions to exotic countries to find and catalogue new types of birds and insects, nor her mother, a strong, intelligent and independent woman in her own right, would have normally hoped their daughter would be swiftly married without first finding the right man and falling in love with him, but now that her father was gone, what remained of the family's fortunes could not possibly last them both forever. Sadly, William Basset, whilst a wonderful father and husband, had not been a rich man and when he was taken by the indiscriminately deleterious consumption, he had yet to fully publish his papers and discoveries that would, he had said, make their fortune.

Millicent's mother had approached the various learned societies William had been a member of, to see if they would take his notebooks, sketches and taxidermic collections of cured, glossy-feathered bird skins and boards of beetles and flies, pinned row up-on iridescent row. Most of these organisations looked kindly upon their brethren's widow and child but, while they paid over the odds for his materials, everyone knew it would never provide an income in the long term.

Jewellery that William had bought his wife, Jacqueline, in happier days was sold, and extraneous servants were let go, in a drive to trim the fat for leaner times.

For the moment, it seemed, there was enough money, but, while her mother tried to reassure her daughter that everything would be al-right, when Millicent challenged her as to where an unsubstantiated superannuation would materialise from, all her mother would say was that she was sure providence could be depended upon, and avoided the young woman's questioning gaze.

It was, in part, because of the fear of an impending life of penury, the threat of the poor house in years to come, or a marriage based solely on practicality and convenience, that Millicent took the initi-ative to generate her own source of income for herself and her remaining parent, and partly because she yearned to be independent and strong, like her father and mother, that she started to engage in the activities that she now found so compelling and difficult to re-nounce.

Her secret activities were inspired by a brief encounter one evening as she made her way home from calling on a friend who lived on High Holborn. The London streets were quiet that autumnal night, but the murky mists combined with the soot and sulphurous smoke from the plenitude of domestic and industrial chimneys, turning the air to thick, yellowish-grey smog, known as a 'pea souper', because of its similarity to the leguminous broth.

Dismissive of any potential threat and eschewing the procurement of a Hackney carriage, Miss Basset boldly chose to walk the mile or so home, to Clerkenwell, unaccompanied, through the dark and smoggy London streets.

Crossing Red Lion Square she became aware that her footsteps were now being dogged by another's, trying to keep in step with hers, heavier-shod and approaching from behind, their sound deadened by the noisome vapours. Gripping the handle of her umbrella more tightly she raised her chin and defiantly strode ahead, increasing her speed in an effort to outpace anyone shadowing her progress. Ducking into the narrow gloom of Lamb's Conduit Passage, in an effort to gain Theobald's Road more swiftly, Millicent was about to emerge from this shortcut, onto Red Lion Street and into the lights and clamour of The Enterprise public house when she found herself cruelly grabbed by the back of her coat collar, hauled back into the alley and pushed against a grimy wall, knocking the breath from her body.

Momentarily stunned by the force of the assault and frozen to inaction with fear she regarded her assailant. He was not a tall man, but was stocky and powerfully built. He had several teeth missing from his upper jaw and the general caste of someone form the lower end of the working classes – perhaps an unskilled labourer. His clothing was oily with filth and the rough mends here and there brought the words of her stern Grandmother to mind, who had once said that, "A tear is an accident that may befall any gentleman, but a patch is premeditated poverty!"

Brought sharply back to the present by the ruffian's sudden and urgent manhandling of her, searching for jewellery around her throat and wrists, and rummaging for money in her chatelaine, Millicent found herself spurred into unexpected action. While the man knew she would have something of value about her person, what he didn't know, and was unlikely to ever have considered, given his masculine prejudices concerning young women, was how her late father had prepared her, and her mother, for eventualities such as an attack like this, here in London, or in one of the many, less civilised, countries they'd visited together.

To explain, let us pause, in our thrilling retelling of this tale, to furnish ourselves with a proper context and understanding of what is about to happen.

As one explorer to another, William Basset had been on friendly terms with Mr Edward Barton-Wright, a keen pugilist who combined English boxing and wrestling with exotic techniques he had learned from Masters of the combative arts in both Europe and the Empire of Japan. The result was a system Mr Barton-Wright later described as "a new art of self defence", which, "when used as it should be, in defending the weak against the strong, would be of great service in those countries where one would not find fair play"[6]. The essence was in learning "clever and tricky techniques" that enable a weaker, lighter opponent to use skill and anatomical mechanics to easily defeat a stronger, heavier opponent. This system was dubbed 'Bartitsu' – a portmanteau word, combining part of the name of its progenitor with part of the word Jiujitsu, a name which the Japanese proponents used to refer to their style of wrestling – and was experimentally taught to Gentlemen enthusiasts, but also to Ladies, as healthy exercise and assurance of their own protection.

Having been enrolled in Mr Barton-Wright's new teaching programme, along with her mother, and practised with such frequency and application as to create unconscious reflexive responses, Millicent Basset took advantage of her foe's clumsy and heavy movements, making use of a skill this man would never have suspected she possessed.

So, let us now return to the scene of conflict in the narrow, dirty and dark alley, to understand quite how the young woman turned the man's brutishness and assumptions against him.

---

[6] From 'A lecture on Jiujitsu and Judo', delivered to the Japan Society of London, February 13th 1901

Stepping back to look her up and down for valuables to steal, the grubby assailant suddenly doubled over in pain as Millicent had, with a two-handed jab, forced the metal ferrule of her umbrella into the thug's solar plexus. Roaring in pain and fury he tried to straighten up, thrusting out his arm, making a grab for her throat. Swiftly, calmly and with elegant precision Millicent pivoted, simultaneously grinding her spiked boot heel into the man's foot and, avoiding the man's lunge and, caught his wrist, pulling his arm to continue his forward lunge. Stepping briskly to the side as he stumbled forward and rather than risk damaging her cultured feminine hands, Millicent abruptly brought up her elbow, contacting hard with the man's jaw as he flew past and into the wall.

Spending only a moment to make sure he was not about to rise and retaliate, the young woman quickly searched the thief for her belongings, before leaving him sprawled on the floor, dazed and confused, stepping smartly into the gas-lit Red Lion Street and hurrying on home.

* * *

Back at home, having avoided conversation with her mother and now taking stock of her recent experience Millicent found she was possessed of a furtive thrill. Not only had she survived what may have been a life-threatening experience, she had triumphed! To yet further augment this success, having emptied the contents of her chatelaine onto her bed she discovered that in addition to recovering her money and jewellery, in the melee she had scooped up two pocket watches that the man had presumably picked from gentlemen's pockets. Her first thought was to find how to return the watches, but then she considered how she might take them to the same shop her mother had sold her jewels at, claim they were her father's and sell them to help support the two of them.

The secrecy, success and the moral quandary kept her awake for most of the night, but when Millicent rose in the morning she was resolved. Life had dealt her a cruel blow and it seemed that providence had, as her mother had hoped, provided.

That morning, after breakfast and contriving an excuse about certain errands, Millicent headed off to Hatton Garden, one of the City of London's most renown areas for jewellers. She tried to conceal her excitement and walk calmly and sedately so as not to arouse suspicion, although from who she wasn't sure. She was glad that the particular jeweller that her mother had gone to, to sell her jewellery had a small shop, discreet and without a clear view from the street. Entering the premises the bell over the door rang and a kindly, smiling old man stood up from behind the counter, where he had been engaged in some piece of repair or construction and bade her a good morning.

Affecting the attitude of a bereft daughter, wringing a handkerchief between her gloved hands, Millicent explained to the man that in the same way her mother had visited him recently, she too had some items of her father's to sell and would the jeweller be kind enough to offer her a good price so that she and her mother could use the money to avoid destitution. After the briefest of examinations of the two watches she was invited through to a private room to discuss the matter.

Occasionally sniffing and dabbing with her handkerchief, Millicent sat and watched as the old man lifted his glasses to peer at the timepieces through his loupe – the lens used to examine minute elements of gems or jewellery – and then he sat back and regarded Millicent thoughtfully, winding his grey beard round his index finger.

The price the jeweller offered Millicent shocked her, and her new-found confidence found its voice, "Why, that is not one third of the price of even some of the more tawdry time pieces in your window! I couldn't possibly sell my father's watches for the amount you suggest!"

"You're quite right, Miss Basset, you shouldn't sell your father's watches for such a small amount", the old man agreed leaning forward, a mischievous smile creasing his face. He opened the case of one of the watches, turning its interior to face her, so she could see the inscription '*To my darling Georgie, from your loving wife Hepsiba*'.

"But these are not your father's watches", the man continued. "And your mother – whose name is certainly not Hepsiba – already sold me your father's watch recently because of the need to support you both".

Suddenly Millicent was afraid and felt trapped. She felt perspiration prickle on her forehead and panic rising in her chest.

The old jeweller sensed her fear and sat back with a placatory, avuncular air. "I don't know where you got these, but I see you didn't own them. You're a nice young lady and I doubt anyone's come to any harm where these came from". The young woman flushed, remembering the unfortunate thief in the alley, not so far from here.

The man continued, leaning forward, dropping his voice to a confidential murmur, "I don't know where these came from and I don't want to know. I'll give you a fair price for these … delicate … items, you can do whatever you want with the money and we'll say no more about it. What do you say, Miss Basset?"

* * *

Of course, Millicent Basset had had no choice, and had taken the money but, on reflection, and, all things considered, events had resolved very satisfactorily. Her next challenge was how to inveigle the extra funds into the family's accounts, which she did by occasionally adding what she hoped were unsuspicious amounts of coins to her mother's cash box, paying for her purchases mostly herself to reduce her requests for any allowance and, when possible, paying in cash rather than on account.

This seemed to work and they had an easier time for a little while and her mother seemed less worried. Then one day a dreaded thing occurred, as her mother informed her that they were to attend a soirée at the house of an old friend of her father's who had a very eligible son.

In the meantime, inspired by her recent success in defending herself by applying the techniques she had learnt from the art of Bartitsu and wishing to distract herself from what she thought of as the forthcoming parade of herself as something not more than stock at a cattle auction, she set about practising in earnest, when she felt sure neither her mother nor her servants would hear the her exertions.

But eventually, the day came and with her mother's help she was groomed and coiffured and perfumed and dressed and bedecked with what little jewellery was left.

The early conversations with Lord and Lady Asquith had been pleasant enough, but Algernon, the eligible, son spent far too much time lounging against the mantelpiece, smirking and theatrically quaffing his drinks. Whether it was some sort of proprietorial smugness or showing off in an effort to impress her she couldn't decide, but feeling her rage building she excused herself and found her way to one of the upstairs cloakrooms where she could splash some cold water on her face to refresh and calm herself.

Having brought her emotions under control she stepped out onto the landing, heading for the stairs, when Algernon appeared from a room and barred her way.

"Well, well. Alone at last, eh?" His cheeks were flushed with drink and he wavered slightly. Millicent tried to dodge round him, but he sidestepped, again blocking her way.

"Please let me through, Mr Asquith", she managed politely, through gritted teeth.

"Oh, I don't think you really want me move, do you? I think you came up here, so I'd follow? To tempt the buyer? Offer a little sample...?". He pushed open the door to the room he'd emerged from – his bedroom. From the where she stood, Millicent could see the corner of a bed, a full-length mirror and his dressing table with various gentleman's grooming equipment and trays of shining, glittering cufflinks and collar studs.

"Come on now", whined the young man. "Don't pretend to be bashful. If I'm going to get you without a proper dowry, I want to make sure I'm getting something worth having", and at this he roughly caught hold of Millicent's forearm and pulled her towards his bedroom.

Without a conscious thought Millicent rotated her forearm, easily popping his grip open and, as he staggered away under his own momentum, followed up with a push to his shoulder that sent him sprawling into his dressing table, bloodying his nose and scattering his carefully ordered trays of cufflinks.

Hurrying downstairs, the young woman arrived back into the drawing room, her cheeks flushed and clearly in a state of excitement. Close behind, was Algernon Asquith, pale faced and a handkerchief held to his bleeding nose. "She hit me", was all he could squeak.

Needless to say, the next few minutes were more than a little awkward, where questions where asked, accusations made and, ultimately, a spoilt young man believed over any argument to the contrary. Millicent and her Mother were asked to leave the house, not to return, which Misses Basset agreed to with ease.

* * *

That night, whilst Millicent felt that she could relax about the matter of enforced marriage, she was still fuming about how she had been used and then discarded and, most of all, not believed, and she was determined to see the Asquith heir punished and an article in the evening's paper had given her rebellious intent food for thought: A cat burglar had started to prey upon certain well-to-do members of London's polite society. Scotland Yard had no leads as to whom he was, as no clues had been left, other than a charismatic calling card, bearing the name *Jack B. Nimble*.

Reminding herself that derring-do should not be the sole preserve of men, an idea her late father and her mother had been careful to instil in her, she determined to have an adventure of her own, seek revenge, and help the family's fortunes at the same time.

Over the next few days, young Millicent Basset bought herself a scandalously figure-hugging costume – actually a male ballet dancer's top and leggings, some fresh ballet shoes and constructed a head covering from a lightweight scarf – all in midnight black, with a plan to take on the guise of Jack B. Nimble and relieve the arrogant Algernon of his cufflinks and any other jewellery; she'd even had some calling cards made bearing the name Jack B. Nimble, simpering and girlishly telling the printer it was for a birthday jape with a friend.

During the day and being sure to be discrete, using a parasol to hide herself, she took walks around Lord and Lady Asquith's house, looking for easy vantage points to gain ingress to the young man's bedroom.

Finally she decided that all her preparations were done and, as evening approached, she told her Mother she was going out to visit a suitable friend, which was fine, as her Mother said she also had to go out on family business and would likely be back late. With the outward composure of a well brought up young lady, but her heart thumping and her hands feeling clammy, she left her home for the night's escapade.

Her dark clothing concealed beneath her day clothes, she walked some way from her house to a small alley she had already chosen for its proximity to the Asquith's house and its suitability for changing her apparel without observation.

The poorly lit streets and the heavy pawl of evening smog were perfect cover for Millicent to turn into the alley as she reached it, without provoking comment. Nervous and checking there were no other occupants, she found the place where she had hidden a slim bundle of tools and, as quickly as fastenings and laces allowed, she stripped off her outer clothing and bundled it into a bag for safe keeping and stowed this in the same place she had removed the tools from. Hand over hand, she was pleased to find that her exercise regime had paid dividends as she climbed a drainpipe and found herself on the roofs of London. Looking across the city, she could see spires and chimney pots stretching into the misty gloaming, the dome of St Paul's Cathedral, less than half a mile away like the back of a great sea beast, breaching the surface of the ocean of miasma. Up here she was alone and free – no one to tell her what to do or who to be – and she began to pick her way over to her target house, lightly springing between roofs and taking run ups and leaping over narrow streets.

The Asquith's house home was a large, detached town house, in the Georgian style, with a mature wisteria climbing its neatly cut stone façade, and surrounded by a wall of about eight feet in height. Lying, stretched out, like a stalking cat, on the edge of the flat roof nearest her prey, Millicent, swathed head to tow in black cloth with only her eyes peeping from a gap in the head scarf checked the surrounding streets for pedestrians. Seeing a gap in the foot traffic and carriages, she slid down another drainpipe, praying it was sturdy and, reaching the ground scuttled to the base of the wall at the side of the Asquith's property, crouching in the shadows, catching her breath and trying not to think too hard about what she was about to do – and was already doing, for that matter.

Listening for another silent and empty moment on the main street, she then slowly stood, faced the wall and sprung up, clutching the edge with her fingertips and painfully pulled herself up so that she was lying, flattened, along the top, panting and surveying the courtyard with its delicately forged and locked iron gate onto the street.

Confident she was unnoticed, Millicent rolled off the wall, landing on her feet and rolling, as her Bartitsu teacher had taught her, to minimize the force of the landing and, in this case, to hide any noise.

The next part was almost too easy as the climbing wisteria presented a very serviceable ladder up to the young man's bedroom, where she found his window already open as if her mother's providence was leading her. A quick glance through the open window, the strong, sweet smell of the creeper's heavy blossoms rinsing any reek of the London streets from her senses, she could see that the room was unoccupied and the bed, made ready for sleep, was empty – likely the smug Lordling was out at one of those gentlemen's clubs she'd heard about, but been denied entry to, on account of her sex, where men drank to excess and gambled and boasted to each other; it crossed her mind that she might be the subject of some conversation and that already, as she clung like a night fiend, to the outside of young Asquith's window, her reputation was being impugned with abandon and washed down with champagne for the entertainment of other ill-behaved young men and this brought a flush of anger that propelled her through the available gap and into the silent room.

For a few moments she allowed herself a break, breathing heavily from the exertion and thrill of it all, listening to the sounds of the house to make sure no one was about to enter. In the darkness and quiet she replayed the events of that recent night and, again felt a flush of anger at how she had been treated – the presumption, the lack of respect, the assault on her person and the cowardly denial.

Now turning her attention to the dressing table, off which she had bounced young Algernon Asquith, Millicent froze and she felt her blood turn to water. The cufflink trays were there but the cufflinks weren't. Nor were the collar studs, the pearl-backed brush, silver comb or, for that matter, anything of relative value that she had seen before. But what there was, was a single calling card, upon which, in elegant curling script was printed the name Jack B. Nimble; she had been beaten to it, by the famous cat burglar himself, and a quiet noise behind her told her that he was still there.

Wheeling around, she saw a figure moving out of the shadows in the corner of the room. He was slight in build and short for most men – ideally suited to his trade. He was also dressed in a remarkably similar style to herself, clad in black, complete with a hood that only allowed a slim letterbox-shaped gap and soft black shoes with a separated big toe, like many she had seen on her travels with her family in the Far East.

The man made a movement towards the window, but Millicent wasn't going to let her prize slip away that easily and, in a couple of bounds had closed with the figure and, as he bent to hurriedly climb out of the window, kicked him in a most unladylike but very effective way in the stomach, producing a stifled gasp. Calling on her combative training Millicent now attacked in earnest, sending flying blows to the burglar's head and body, but found herself surprised as, after a particularly successful and hard strike to her opponent's face, the masked man turned and began to deftly block and evade further blows, finishing by returning a similar cuff to the young woman's cheek, sending her staggering back a few paces in a moment of dizziness and giving the man time to tumble through the open window and into the London night.

By the time she reached the window, Jack B. Nimble was up and over the perimeter wall and lost in the city.

Exhilarated by the bout, but crestfallen by the failure to exact her own revenge on the house of Asquith, Millicent judiciously decided that tonight's foray was over and, touching what she feared was a rising bruise under one eye, followed the lead of the cat burglar and slipped out into the night, retracing her steps home and hurried to bed before her mother could come to her room.

* * *

The next morning Millicent Basset was horrified to look in the mirror on her own dressing table and see her eye had puffed up so that it was almost closed and was surrounded by skin, most moribund, in colours of dark greens and blue-blacks. Pacing her bedroom, she realised she couldn't conceal the injury – the only sort of makeup that would hide it was the sort worn by actresses, or women of reputations she shuddered to be associated with. In the end she concocted a tale of foolish girlish parlour frolics with her spurious chum, involving a table tennis paddle and larks gone wrong. Steeling herself to deliver the lie, she dressed and went down to breakfast.

On entering the breakfast room, her excitement got the better of her and immediately she saw her mother, seated, facing away from her at the breakfast table. She gave a brittle and overly bright *Good morning!*, making her mother jump a little. Instantaneously and simultaneously both women began blurting out stories of the previous night and how they had both had humorously silly accidents and, rounding the edge of the table, Millicent and her mother both looked upon each other and fell suddenly silent regarding each other's swollen and bruised faces.

"You!" they both said at once.

And there, spread out on the breakfast table in front of the older woman was the morning's paper, telling of another scurrilous robbery – this time of the unfortunate son of Lord Asquith – by the mysterious and enigmatic gentleman cat burglar, Jack B. Nimble.

* * *

Over kippers and coffee Millicent's mother, Jacqueline Basset – or 'Jack B.' – as she had chosen to call herself to disguise her activities, told how she had chosen families of people who had promised subscriptions to her late husband's work, but when their hour of need had come they'd changed their minds and left the widow and her daughter with rapidly dwindling finances. This last robbery was unusual in that, for the same reasons as Millicent, Jacqueline Basset had sought revenge for the wronging of her daughter and it was mere coincidence – if such a thing exists – that both had chosen the same night. Both remarked on how William Basset's real legacy of two adventurous and independent women had resulted in them dueling over the spoils of righteous plunder.

After serious consideration, it was decided that Jack B. Nimble would not die that morning and that he would continue his nocturnal shenanigans, but from now on he would also have a rather Robin Hood caste to his activities in that as well as bolstering the family fortunes, this elusive man would not only select particularly worthy – or unworthy, depending on your point of view – targets, but also contribute some of the profits to needy causes.

And so, under the story of selling exotic treasures gathered by the late William Basset, and some prudent investment of the same, two respectable Victorian ladies were able pass, unsuspected, whist operating as a cat burgling jewel thief – a man known by his enigmatic calling card of Jack B. Nimble, and live out their lives as they wished: Mrs Jacqueline Basset became the patron of a number charities and sat on numerous committees for the improvement of London and those who lived within its confines, while Miss Millicent Basset was a young woman of independent means and significant learning, who *did* get married, but only when she had found a man *she* deemed suitable.

Jack B. Nimble was never caught, but after a while his activities dwindled and eventually stopped altogether and the 'man' was never caught, nor 'his' real identity ever suspected.

Four Knaves, No Man's Land, Western Europe

P rivate Buck – William Buck, known as Jack – shouldn't have been there, but there he was and within a whisker of losing his life. His tin helmet had stopped him from being killed outright, but, with a bleeding head wound, stars popping in front of his eyes mimicking the lightning-bright blasts from the shells screaming around him, and feeling the thunder of their explosions shaking his young body, he teetered on the lip of a bomb hole before his knees gave way, and he pitched forward, rolling down into the soft mud at the base of the newly formed crater, and the world went silent and black.

* * *

Aged fifteen and a year or so into his apprenticeship as a ship-wright in Southampton, Jack had felt it was high time he went off to be a man and *bash the Bosch*, and so, ignoring the army's minimum age limit of eighteen, he lied about his own age and joined the Hampshire Regiment to go and fight overseas for King and Country.

Today was to be the glorious day when he and the other lads went 'over the top' and beat the Kaiser's army back to where they belonged. But it hadn't quite gone the way he and the others had imagine it.

After basic training in Blighty and hearing and reading about how well it was going on the continent, Jack and the other new recruits were all hungry for some action. Even the journey by boat over the channel, with plenty of them emptying their breakfasts over the sides, hadn't dulled their enthusiasm.

However, after landing, things suddenly became darker than he'd expected. The muck and the dirt was nothing to worry about – to begin with at least – but the doubts started on seeing the rows and rows of wounded, lying side by side at the edges of the roads like so many fish in a fishmonger's window. Some had simple slings or bandages, but others had arms and legs missing, were yelling in pain or delirium and, as he watched, some were covered with their sheets, now beyond the help of the doctors and nurses. Other men, returning from the front, had expressions on their faces that chilled him: eyes hollow and staring, their cheekbones gaunt and all of them so very, very quiet. Here there was very little of the glory and glamour of battle that he'd heard and dreamt about. The bands and banners were all back in England whereas here was carnage and the waste of a very different war machine. It was hard to believe that they were winning at all.

Last of all, even at this distance of many days' travel away from the front, he could hear the low grumble and thumping giant's footsteps of bombardment – ours or theirs? Both, apparently.

* * *

The busy port was now far behind them. As the trucks drove them closer to the front, the landscape became more and more barren. Buildings became fewer and fewer and those that still stood were just ruins: skeletal timbers and crumbled walls where once a farm or hotel, or even, on one occasion, a whole village had stood, now blown to bricks and splinters.

Eventually the road became so much a mixture of potholes and mud that the wheeled vehicles – some military build, some civilian vans and even buses, conscripted and painted olive drab – could go no further. From this point, only men, horses and the monstrous tanks he'd only ever heard about, could cross the ravaged ground.

When they reached the trenches, plunging calf-deep into freezing, liquid mud, the squalor finally dowsed the young men's enthusiasm. They were welcomed by the veterans already there, who told them the best ways they'd learned to stay as comfortable as possible in the conditions, and were keen to trade things for news from home, fresh rations and cigarettes. After all, why would the new boys need them – they were *all* going over the top at dawn and it was likely that none of them were coming back.

No one got the good night's sleep they needed, as shells continued to rain down like an unending storm of falling stars, shaking the ground with deep thumps, as if two mighty titans were fighting, hand-to-hand, just out of sight in the darkness. Unable to sleep, Jack stepped outside and joined the men on watch in case of a German sneak attack. Indolently, the soldiers leaned against the trench walls, eking out their cigarettes, sharing one between many to avoid lighting another and running out. The darkness of the night was absolute, broken by pools of orange from paraffin lamps, set out at distances from each other. But then, for a moment, it would be bright as a summer's day as a shrieking shell exploded, bringing everything into sudden, sharp relief.

Jack borrowed a periscope from one of the watchmen and peered over the top of the sandbags. It was a crude, tall wooden box with angled mirrors top and bottom and covered in scuffed green paint, but peeping over the top of the trench, in the intermittent bursts of white light Jack could see a landscape that looked more like the surface of the moon so blasted were the fields and meadows. Curiously, there was no sign of the enemy who were sending bombs and sniper's bullets, and its sterile, hellish emptiness filled him with a fear that came from the sudden realisation of the truth.

* * *

Just before dawn the next day Jack and his fellow new recruits tightened the chin straps on their helmets, fixed bayonets, and stood at the foot of ladders, waiting for the signal. The men were silent; every one of them part of a greater force, yet alone with their thoughts, their fears and their prayers. Nearby their officers repeatedly checked their timepieces and toyed with whistles, chained to their breast pockets.

And then silence descended.

The great guns that pounded the enemy day and night stopped and the world changed from a devilish, clamorous pandemonium to a dreadful, awful quiet.

Nervously, soldiers shuffled their feet and began to look expectantly at the officers, or up at the tops of the ladders, hitching their rifles on their shoulders.

An age seemed to pass and then, as the second hands on their watches ticked towards the twelve, officers slowly brought the whistles to their lips. As the first hour of dawn struck, shrill blasts were blown and hundreds upon hundreds of brave lads scrambled up the ladders and ran.

From the base of the ladders, waiting his turn, all Jack could see was man after man climbing up and disappearing over the top of the trench. Quickly a bestial roar rose from the collective throats of the charging men, breaking the silence and, as that heroic cry grew in volume and in courage, only a few moments passed before it was answered by the rattling chatter of machineguns and enemy rifles.

How could they be so close, yet Jack hadn't seen them last night? But dug in and invisible in their own trenches, the Germans had made ready for the charge as soon as the allied bombardment had ceased – giving them the signal that attack was imminent.

Now, his turn, automatically propelled to follow his brothers in arms, Jack scuttled up the ladder and over the top.

In the daylight the land was no less alien: Patches of turf were here and there, but No Man's Land, the area that he and thousands of others ran screaming across, was mostly churned mud, strewn with barbed wire and debris. But, whereas last night the land had been empty it was now filled with men, running like ants, jumping over the bodies of their comrades and friends, lying dead or dying, and running straight towards where enemy machineguns spat fire and threw hot lead that brought down man after man after man, from the distant safety of trenches and heaps of sandbags.

Next to him, and just in front, a man he'd trained with and drunk with was roaring with savage fury and running full tilt, bayonetted rifle held out before him, like a lance, only for Jack to see his back suddenly threaded by a string of red beads. The man silently dropped, motionless and mute in the mud. All the men around him were dropping - dropping like the table skittles in the pub his Dad liked to drink in – but futilely the rest carried on, and as they did, more and more fell silent, to the clatter and rattle of enemy guns.

Realising it was only a matter of time before he too fell under the spraying bullets, Jack decided to take shelter in a bomb hole. As he headed onwards, forwards, he spotted a deep, fresh crater and pushed himself even harder to get there faster. Feeling something – a bullet – pass, searing hot and cutting across his shoulder, he ignored it, mounting the lip of the crater. Moments, mere parts of a second before he was to gain cover, he felt another bullet hit his head, ringing loudly off his metal helmet, stunning him with the force and shock of the ricochet. He staggered for a moment, confused, before passing out and falling forward, into the safety of the crater.

* * *

It was dark when Jack opened his eyes. Lying on his back, he stared up at the beautiful galaxy of stars, peacefully twinkling in the heavens and wondered if he was dead.

Turning his head to look around him, fresh stars burst in front of his eyes, caused by the earlier impact of the bullet. When his vision had cleared, and he could see by the starlight, he saw there were others in the crater. Most of them were definitely dead, but in one corner sat three figures, close together. One was an officer – a Lieutenant – the others simple Privates, like him. One of the Privates was coughing wretchedly, hacking away, and looked ill – dreadfully ill – surely unfit for active service; the other looked half starved and was repeatedly picking up now empty tins and used a grubby finger to try and scrape out any last remaining traces of food.

It was quiet. There was no bombardment, no gunfire. No sound – not of anyone, living, anywhere.

As he struggled to sit up the Lieutenant turned and smiled. "Ah! We thought you'd already bought it. Never too late for a second chance, eh? That's the ticket."

It was friendly gallows humour and Jack was glad of the company and to have someone in charge, but something about the officer made him uneasy - his skin was a little too pale and his grin a little too toothy and it felt like your eyes slid off him if you tried to look too long.

"Come on over and join us". It was more of a statement than a suggestion, even a command, and Jack crawled over, making sure to avoid getting anywhere near making himself a target for an enemy sniper.

"Private Buck, Sir", Jack clipped to the officer who nodded, removing a deck of cards from a pocket and beginning to shuffle.

"Jack. That's what people call you isn't it?"

"Yes, Sir. Do I know you, Sir?"

"Oh, I think you probably do, Jack", grinned the Lieutenant. "I certainly know you".

And at that point, the pain became too much and Jack slipped away again into blessed oblivion, at least for a while.

When Jack woke the second time it was to the sound of the wracking coughs from the other soldier who was shivering and sweating, rocking backwards and forwards as the other man gnawed on a leather belt. It was still dark but a moment later someone sent up a flare, lighting up the surroundings with a ghostly glow. Jack took a swig from the officer's hip flask, feeling instantly revived by the strong, burning liquid and accepted a cigarette from the man, taking a slow drag and feeling his head spin as he looked around the crater at the white faces of his fallen brethren, staring sightlessly at the heavens.

"What say you to a game?" The Lieutenant started shuffling the cards again, and Jack mutely nodded. He'd been looking at the officer's uniform and realised he didn't recognise the insignia on his cap badge – four horses, their manes and tails flying as they ran.

"Sorry, Sir", he began. "I don't think I got your name or which regiment you're with.

The Lieutenant answered, but even though he asked again, Jack somehow couldn't seem to hold the man's name in his head – the concussion must have been bad, but he understood from what he was saying, that he and the others – the hungry and the sickly man – were normally part of some cavalry outfit and that there was another of their group who was around somewhere.

Jack looked wearily at the two hands of cards the Lieutenant had set out on the remains of a wooden crate.

"Let's play your name sake, shall we? Spot of Black Jack?" Jack explained that he didn't know how to play but the officer hushed him and said he'd teach him and afterwards he'd let Jack suggest a game.

"What shall we play for, eh?" asked the Lieutenant, grinning, his teeth and skin shining under the chemical light of the flair.

"I've not got anything except for the clothes I sit in – and they're not mine – just them and the soul God gave me."

"Well then, let's see what we can do with that, eh?" chuckled the man and they started to play.

Jack felt he was slipping in and out of consciousness, nodding as he laid and picked up cards, but the game continued until the Lieutenant declared he had won and Jack lost, and warned the young man to pick his game carefully as this would be the last chance they'd have to play.

In his sleepy, daze, Jack remembered a magician he'd seen on stage in Southampton and how he'd been enraptured by the man's theatricality and tricks, even pulling a gold coin from Jack's ear. As well as tugging his own ear all the way home to try and find another coin, he'd later got a book out of the library and learned some tricks himself, including the sleight of hand involved in 'Find the Lady'.

Feeling like his fingers were thick and unresponsive as sausages, Jack still laid out two cards face up – the Jack of Hearts and the Jack of Spades – and then between them put the Queen of Hearts. Next he flipped them over, moved them around and turned the Queen face up, to confirm to the officer where she was. Turning her face down again he swapped, turned, mixed and moved the cards. The officer, however, watching with what appeared now to be a permanently fixed grin, chuckled and pointed at the card he *knew* to be 'The Lady'. With a dazed, lazy motion of his hand, Jack motioned for him to turn the card over, knowing that he had used his skills to misdirect the man into thinking he had been following the correct card.

The officer flipped the card and started, gasping a sharp intake of breath; the card he'd chosen was not 'The Lady', but was, instead, the Jack of Hearts.

The man laughed out loud, congratulating Jack on his success. Maybe it was the officer clapping in appreciation or maybe the machineguns had started up again, but the man stood up, gathering the deck of cards.

"Well, Private. It looks like we'll have to postpone our final game for another time. I must say I wasn't expecting that – I'm not often beaten; I'll have to look out for you next time, Jack", he grinned. "For now, though, it's over the top with the others".

The sound of guns was certainly very real now, from both in front and behind. A smoke screen had been set off somewhere and was now drifting over and into the bomb hole, covering the advance of the British troops over the flair-lit ground.

"I'm not sure I can, Sir", groaned Jack, being hauled to his feet by the officer.

"Nonsense", said the man. "I think you're going to be just fine. Here", he said, stuffing the pack of cards into Jack's left breast pocket. "Take these for good luck. Now, off you go", and, thrusting his rifle into his hands, he pushed Jack up and over the lip of the bomb hole into the blinding, opaque smoke, surrounded by the feral shouts of the soldiers, the cries of the wounded and the blasting, flashing staccato from the enemy emplacements.

For a moment he wavered, feeling as if eternity were spinning like a coin on a table and then solid hits to his body sent him reeling back into the crater and back into unconsciousness.

* * *

Private William 'Jack' Buck came round a number of times – on a stretcher with someone shouting something into his face, then in a truck with a muddy medic smiling down at him and muttering comforting things, and later on what felt like a boat – but each time he sank down into the depths of unconsciousness and dream, before finally waking properly in a sunlit bed, with clean white sheets and in a ward with other convalescing soldiers.

During his recuperation he was visited by the Military Police, who'd found out his real age, and when he was well enough and had recovered, he was handed over to the regular police where, after being sentenced by a magistrate, he spent a further two weeks in jail for breaking the terms of his apprenticeship.

It was only a nominal sentence, a slap on the wrist, seeing as he'd shown courage and loyalty to King and Country by enlisting, even if he had been underage.

Jack returned to his work as an apprentice shipwright – light duties to begin with – and when he was of age, he was disappointed that he was found 'not fit for active duty' and denied a commission, much to his frustration.

After he was married and his children were old enough, he would tell and retell them the story of his night in No Man's Land, and when his children said they didn't believe him, as they always did, he would sigh theatrically and have to prove his story by getting his memento of that night: A deck of cards, the first four all the Jacks, the topmost visible card the Jack of Hearts and perfectly pierced and still held together by a German machinegun bullet.

Epilogue

When I finished telling this final story I looked up, feeling as if I had just woken from a deep, dream-filled sleep; the sun was setting and I was famished.

Kleiou was nowhere to be seen, and the framed pictures and papers had gone from the walls.

But the furniture was all there: I was still sitting in the same chair and in front of me was a table with a, now empty, ceramic goblet.

Immediately, I plugged my laptop in and, yes, there was power, and so wrote all that I could remember – this collection of stories is the result.

A few hours before dawn I slept fitfully, curled up on the sofa and when I woke a little later, early the next day, I explored the villa and its grounds, quiet in their emptiness and in the chill of the morning, before the Italian sun had risen over the tops of the high hedges.

On the journey back, across boundaries, across oceans, passing in and out of border controls, the idea of nations and nationalism now felt absurd as I looked back down the long line of my own ancestors who had crossed land and sea and at each place they stopped and lived and loved and brought new life into the world – that place was home.

Looking into the faces of my fellow passengers and the people I passed in the streets I forgot my own worries and modern anxieties for a moment and wondered what each of their stories might be and what were the stories they carried in their blood.

We all have our own stories – no matter how big or how small – to tell or to treasure, and we are all the perfected versions our ancestors sought to make.

Whether it was some sort of mental aberration that led me to an empty house in another country, or that I was summoned there by a Muse who had given a good life, good luck and a desire for adventure to an ancient ancestor of mine and all his descendants, I'm not sure, but, as a storyteller I know is often fond of saying…

"All stories are true … some of them even happened".

Ω

#0112 - 221018 - C0 - 210/148/9 - PB - DID2335913